THE LOST COAST

THE LOST COAST

A JEFF TAYLOR MYSTERY

Scott Lipanovich

Encircle Publications
Farmington, Maine, U.S.A.

Editor, Encircle Publications: Cynthia Brackett-Vincent
Cover design by Christopher Wait
Cover images © Getty Images

Published by:

Encircle Publications
PO Box 187
Farmington, ME 04938

info@encirclepub.com
http://encirclepub.com

Printed in U.S.A.

To the memory of Roy C. Lipanovich and John C. Brosnan,
who overcame extreme adversity without complaint.

One

A rural highway led to a ridge high above the Pacific Ocean. I pulled over, climbed out of my car and stretched. Nine a.m., the Saturday of Labor Day weekend, I was far up the northern California coast. Mossy forest ran downhill to the ribbon-like road that followed the shoreline. The ocean, coated with fog, seemed to hover beneath a sky the color of milk. I'd driven halfway across the state to do something I didn't want to do.

For three years I'd been doing things I didn't want to do. I'd finally quit, just the previous Wednesday. I had no plan. All I knew with certainty was I needed to make a new start in life. Looking down into fog and clouds, I thought it only right I help my ex-boss with a last favor. Clint Sherman had faithfully watched me play basketball during my undergrad years at Sacramento State, his alma mater, and later hired me when I was without job prospects. More important, he'd lifted me from a downward spiral of physical pain and self-pity.

Saturday at three-thirty in the morning, Clint called with news that his long-time poker buddy, state Senator Allan Watkins, had been charged with driving while intoxicated and vehicular manslaughter. Clint asked me to drive west and north to post bail. So there I was, stretching my limbs, looking at the crowns of redwood trees.

The road took me down through the trees. I then drove up the coast to Sunset, a village of brightly painted wood buildings and old cottages converted into ocean-view rentals. On the inland side of the highway, an office complex housed the various arms of Sunset County government. Few cars were in the parking lot. Rubbing my hands together—well, rubbing my left hand and half a right hand together against cold morning dampness—I walked to the glass entrance doors of the Sheriff's Office.

A confident-looking young woman about my age, twenty-five, was behind the front counter. Most of her brown hair was tucked beneath a dark patrolman's cap. A nameplate identified her as *Anne Simpson, Clerk*. She said, "May I help you?"

"My name's Jeff Taylor. I'm here to take care of the senator's bail." I took out my wallet, set it on the high counter, and opened it to show my driver's license.

"Of course," Anne said, though she suddenly seemed uncertain. She gave my license a cursory glance. Behind her, the dispatch radio crackled. Anne flinched.

My right hand is missing the two smallest fingers. The middle finger is a stump that doesn't rise to the occasion of flipping someone the bird. Its hideousness is the reason I didn't go to medical school. Its weakened capacity is the reason I didn't play pick-up ball anymore. The only thing useful to come from that chopped hand was learning that by exposing it I usually gained people's sympathies.

Anne went to a drawer, took out two forms and brought them to the counter. "You didn't go through a bondsman, right? That's what I was told. I hope you know we can't take a personal check."

From my left pocket I pulled a wad of bills, hundreds and five hundreds, that totaled ten thousand dollars. The money came from the safe at Sherman Investigations, where I'd met Clint at four a.m. Anne frowned at all the cash. It did look somewhat dirty and somehow morally tainted. Anne unfolded, stacked and then counted to ten thousand as I tried to cover my unreadable signature on the forms she'd presented.

Anne locked the money in a drawer. She gave me copies of what

I'd signed, and the senator's release form. "This is your receipt. Don't lose it."

"What kind of shape is he in? I'm supposed to drive him to wherever he's staying."

"You'll have to decide that for yourself." Anne opened a half door at the end of the counter. The door locked with a *click* as she closed it behind her. We started down a dimly lighted hallway.

I said, "Did you know the guy who got hit? If you don't mind me asking. It's just that it's a small town and all."

"He was way ahead of me in school, but I knew him. Joe Garston. He was always getting in trouble. But he was all right in his own way." Our footsteps broke the silence of the empty hallway. "At least before he became the town drunk."

"How old was he?"

"Thirty-two going on sixteen."

Anne stopped at a tall wood door with CONFERENCE printed on it in white letters. "Well, good luck."

Anne grabbed the doorknob. Instead of turning it, she let go and clasped my left arm at the elbow. In an anxious whisper, she said, "I saw you play. Whatever happened, I'm really, really sorry."

Her chin dipped and Anne walked quickly back down the hallway. I watched until she disappeared around a corner, and shunted any feelings regarding what Anne had said. I'd had ample practice at shunting feelings. I pushed open the door and stepped into the room.

Allan and Marci Watkins sat at a long wooden table. He was slumped over, head in his hands. I saw silvery hair and blocky shoulders. Marci Watkins, who looked to be in her late sixties, stood and offered her right hand.

"You must be the young man Clint Sherman sent." Her long gray hair draped to the middle of her back. Marci wore an oversized purple sweater, purple sweatpants that could have doubled as slacks, and pinkish running shoes. "Thanks for coming."

I shook her hand. Marci blinked at seeing mine. To distract her, I handed Marci the forms I'd signed.

Senator Watkins, drifting out of a shallow sleep, raised his head. His eyes were red. They squinted. He appeared older than his seventy years. "Goddamn it." His voice rose. It was scratchy, like sandpaper crossing wood. "Get me out of here."

I said, "Bail's been posted. You're free to go. The prelim hearing is set for Tuesday morning."

Watkins rose slowly, finding his bearings. I had to be careful not to stare because other than the white Arrow shirt and razor-cut hair, Allan Watkins looked like an old bum roused from the sidewalk by morning traffic. Deep lines scored his forehead in every direction. The eyebrows were white, wild, bare in spots like those of an old bird. His nose was boozer all the way, with red humps and veins splotching its tip.

Watkins raised both hands and flipped them outward. "Stupidest damn thing I ever heard of. No O-R?" He was angry at not being released on his own recognizance. "I've been vacationing in the same house here for twenty years. I'm running a very public campaign in the ninth senatorial district." Watkins looked to the ceiling, shook his silvery head. "Where am I going to go, Mars?"

Marci took his elbow. She steered him toward the door. "C'mon, Honey."

Watkins swerved off course and shook my hand. If he noticed it was only half a hand, he didn't let on. I don't think he noticed. He smelled of sweat and stale liquor.

I said, "I'm Jeff Taylor. Clint Sherman says to tell you he'll get you anything you need."

Watkins said, "It's all a big mistake." His red eyes blinked with fatigue and irritation. "Somebody's got to figure this thing out."

"Let's get you home first."

I walked outside with one of the most powerful elected officials in the state. Among California political junkies, Allan Watkins enjoyed near mythic status as the last of the Heartland Liberals, a man who came to government when Ronald Reagan was still president. The senator drew in deep breaths of fresh air. Every movement of his body was slightly exaggerated, as if he were performing in front of an audience. With his car impounded, the three of us got into my dark blue Volkswagen Jetta. Marci sat next to me; Watkins stretched out in back. We headed north. Thin bands of fog blew over the road and were melted by sunlight as the fog hit inland hills.

Watkins cleared his throat. "I've got a rental coming over from Ukiah. It should be here by noon." He shifted his weight around on the back seat. "This'll get straightened out, Honey. But we have to get on it quick, before the internet nuts get going." He cleared his throat again. "I don't even want to think about what they'll make up. Hell, those screwballs—"

His voice broke into a run of dry coughs.

I took the opportunity to say, "I'm supposed to find out if you've been in contact with Mr. Marquardt."

Thomas Marquardt. The senator's attorney.

Watkins swallowed, snuffed out a last cough. "He's up in the Arctic, on some goddamn nature thing. No cell reception. His assistant is contacting the company he paid to go get his ass froze." Watkins' raspy voice sounded like a growl. "The son of a bitch better be able to do something."

The highway turned away from the ocean. Marci Watkins seemed serene. I wondered: how many times had she been in a car with her husband smelling like a bum? We came out of a turn. The road opened up, then became sharp curves again.

Watkins said, "*Hey.*" I glanced back. Senator Watkins pointed inland. He jabbed at the window with one hand while hitting the button to lower it with the other. His face flashed red and pink. "Son, pull over. Goddamn it pull over!"

I thought he was going to puke. He sure looked like it. I found room to stop safely off the pavement. Watkins flipped the door handle, lurched out, headed back along the dirt shoulder of the road. Tight next to the Jetta was a steep grassy hillside. About forty yards up the hill, a dense weaving of bushes

Watkins stumbled. Wrinkled slacks hung low on his hips, the white shirt was untucked and darkly soiled. Ripping both hands back through silvery hair, he yelled over the wind. "I'm telling you, he came out of nowhere!" Hunched over, Watkins swiveled around and faced Marci and me; we'd left the car and followed him. Watkins took a swing at the sky and shouted something unintelligible.

I spoke quietly to Marci Watkins. "I don't think you want him out in public like this."

Senator Watkins got down on his knees. He ran his right hand through the roadside grass. A car passed. Watkins looked up. The people in the car stared at him. Another passing car honked and swerved. Watkins kept crawling, his face a foot above the ground.

Marci Watkins' eyes showed no strain. "He swears that boy just appeared in the middle of the road. He's not lying. At least not consciously. I'd be able to tell."

I was fascinated by the sight of the legendary state senator groveling on hands and knees. It froze me. Then I realized the calm demeanor of Marci Watkins was the result of extreme fatigue, and likely shock. She passively watched her husband crawl toward a blind curve.

"Senator!" I ran along the shoulder of the road to him. "Senator. Why don't we have a look around?"

If there had been any evidence other than blackish blood stains on pavement, the police surely would have removed it. Still, I went through the motions of helping Watkins search the immediate area. After, I guided him away from the accident site. We sat on the hillside, on yellow, late-summer grass. Cars swooshed by. Watkins trembled. I asked him to recount what happened the night before. I kept my stumpy hand hidden so as not to distract him.

Watkins said Marci picked him up in the capitol's underground parking garage. He'd been negotiating compromises round the clock, and the only thing he wanted was to get the hell out of Sacramento without being cornered by a reporter. Marci drove. It took a couple of hours for him to unwind, but he finally fell asleep.

"Marci woke me when we got to the cabin. She was wiped out from the drive. She went straight to bed. But I'd slept two–three hours. Now I'm wide awake."

Watkins rocked and trembled. "I couldn't quit thinking about some of the things we passed. In these grind-it-out sessions, they always sneak a dirty turkey past you."

Watkins said he'd decided to read some of the bills he voted on, more than six hundred in two days. "Thinking about a few of them got me worked up. I needed to get out, have a drink and unwind. I drove to town, to this place I go called The Cove." Watkins blew out harshly, and cleared his throat. "I sipped a—wait, it was two gin and tonics. I sat there reading till they were about to close. I went out to my car and headed back."

"That would be about two, right?"

Watkins nodded. The left side of his face spasmed, from just under his left ear to the edge of his mouth, tugging at puffy skin. Below us, a car accelerated out of the turn. Its tires sprayed brown dust across Joe Garston's blood stains.

Watkins said, "I was finally enjoying myself. You got to remember, I don't get much time alone, so driving up the coast is a treat. I'm taking peeks at the moon showing on the water." Watkins quit rocking, and pointed. "I go into the turn. I look at the ocean. I come out of the turn and this guy's in my lane. I mean, he's just, he's just *there*."

The senator made waving motions I took to indicate the young man, hitting him, the whole catastrophe. Strands of whitish hair fell across his eyes. "I stopped and ran over to check on him. I…"

Watkins sagged forward onto yellow grass. He vomited. I reached for him, instinctively, but pulled back. I wasn't sympathetic. The man was known to be a major-league boozer. Accounts of his nocturnal escapades abounded in Sacramento. They'd seemed comical when retold in a bar or at a party. Now he had killed someone while driving. Watkins wiped away spittle with the sleeve of the dirty white shirt, coughed and spit a couple of times. His red eyes met mine, and for a few, slow-ticking seconds, he looked as if he might break into tears. The self-dramatist was in genuine pain.

"Senator, I'm sorry you had to go through that." I was just doing my job, or more accurately, my ex-job. Who I really felt sorry for was the guy who got killed.

Marci, who had hung back, climbed the hillside. She reached for him. "Allan, Honey, you've got to get some rest."

He grabbed her hand as if it were a lifeline. Below, a pickup truck roared by.

He said, "I can get up. Give me a minute."

Marci's eyes moved about, unable to settle on any one thing. Finally, they settled on me. "Could you find a place to stay? Clint said you were available. We're going to need some help."

Early that morning, on the long drive, I kept thinking about how much I'd come to detest being Clint Sherman's gofer, and I would be through with all that by noon. But what the hell was another day, when I now had endless days to map out for myself? The senator's vulnerability caused me to see him in a different light. There was no reason I couldn't stay and help until his own people took over.

Pulling on the senator's elbow, I got him to his feet, and kept my grip tight. Marci took the other arm. The three of us descended to the side of the highway. We walked to my car with my good hand clamped to the senator's arm, guiding him. The whole trip was about eighty feet but seemed farther because the senator's steps grew heavier as we proceeded. I near lifted him into the back seat. Watkins looked like he was a hundred years old. The effort of getting back to the car had brought sweat to his tired face. I started the engine and continued up the coast highway.

Marci said, "Drop us by the cabin, then please go. I've got to get him to bed."

Checking the rear-view mirror, I saw Watkins slumped against the door. His eyes were closed. We drove north till Marci directed me to take a long uphill lane that was more like a private road than a driveway.

Eyes still closed, Watkins said, "Jesus Christ. It just hit me: I knew that boy's father. Not well, but I knew him a long time ago."

The senator didn't elaborate. We reached our destination. Marci took him inside without assistance.

Two

I descended the lengthy asphalt driveway and parked before reaching the highway. I called Clint Sherman. I told him Marci Watkins had asked me to find a place to spend the night. "The senator's in disarray. She's probably afraid he'll go on a bender. I'll try to keep him out of view till staff arrives. Any word about that?"

Clint said, "We're working on it. Ping me right away if something comes up."

I called motels and resorts until I found one with a Friday no-show. I rented a studio cabin for one hundred and fifty dollars a night by reciting my credit card number. I drove south, passing through Sunset. Tourists flocked to breakfast. Antiques were being transferred from inside a shop to the sidewalk. The sky cleared and the brightly painted buildings shone. A mile outside of town, on the ocean side of the highway, I found Greenwood, a tall, apple-green Victorian B and B with burgundy trimmings. I went inside, scrawled my name a couple of times and walked out to my car with a key to a studio cabin on a sandy mesa above the gray sea.

After sleeping a couple of hours, I showered and changed into a long-sleeved pullover. Long sleeves made my bad hand less conspicuous. I looked in the mirror and combed my hair, gazing a tad longer than usual. I was leaving Sherman Investigations on a high note. I was calling on Senator Allan Watkins and Mrs. Marci Watkins, at their request.

In town I stopped at Sunset General, bought a couple of protein bars and ate them while driving north. At the Watkins' rental abode, I parked next to a squeaky-clean bronze Ford Taurus. A Hertz sticker was pasted on its back bumper. Wood stairs led to a cedar-shingled house too large to accurately be called a cabin. Marci Watkins opened the door. Her gray hair was in two lengthy braids. She motioned for me to come inside.

The senator sat at a table in the kitchen, talking on a cell phone. I knew he'd gotten decent sleep because his face did not look haggard, and he wasn't squinting. Clean shaven, he wore an aqua polo shirt, brown cords and a pair of white boating shoes. In front of him rested a tumbler, empty except for melting ice.

Watkins smiled and waved to me while speaking into the phone. "Yes, that's my point... That's all we're asking for... Goodbye."

Watkins clicked the phone, set it on the table, then took the glass with him to a couch in the woodsy living room. He blinked, drawing together wrinkles and white eyebrows. "I'm calling people and giving them a last workover before they hear about it. Some already have."

I eased onto a black leather recliner, took in cedar walls, puffy long couches, a granite fireplace that exuded the pleasant smell of wood smoke, and cathedral ceilings that gave the room a lot of air space. The very idea of privilege was expressed in the design of that house. It was as stately as the redwood trees outside and seemed in contradiction to the circumstances that brought me there. And what crap: Watkins killed a guy with his car early in the morning, and here he was practicing politics in the afternoon.

Watkins sucked drops from his glass, sat back. "This is an awkward position for me." His voice trailed off. He set the glass down and nodded thoughtfully at nothing.

Marci had gone into the kitchen. She brought back a wooden platter of sliced cheddar cheese and Club crackers, and a tumbler of mineral water. Her long gray braids bounced, mirroring light steps.

Marci set the food and water on a pine coffee table. She said, "Our kids are in Hawaii with their families. We don't want them involved any sooner than necessary. We want to thank you and Clint for coming through for us."

"Not a problem." As far as I could tell, so far Marci hadn't lied to me. This impressed me a great deal.

Marci looked from me to the senator, and back, as though taking measure. She said, "Now's probably a good time to run to the market. Before the press shows up and I can't go outside without getting cornered."

Watkins eyed my full glass of water. "Good idea. Yeah." He tapped his empty tumbler on the coffee table. To me, he said, "It's like war, digging in with rations before battle."

Marci said, "Okay, let's get it over with."

She marched off. It was obvious Marci was uncomfortable leaving, knowing Watkins might drink, but she probably figured it was better to leave with me around to look after him. I attacked the crackers and cheese. It struck me that I'd be hanging around until Watkins fetched his team back from Labor Day weekend getaways. That could take a day or two. I didn't look forward to babysitting Watkins, but knew handling a situation this delicate would bring a thousand bucks, or more, a welcome bonus. I made a mental note to hike up behind the house and see what trails and such could allow nosy reporters or photographers access.

Watkins leaned forward. "Son, let's put things on the table." The empty tumbler automatically went to his mouth; he tipped it, set the glass down. "It's no secret I've had a few incidents involving alcohol. Maybe you read about the time I hit a guardrail coming back into town. Papers had a ball with that one. Back in '16 I plead no contest to having an open container in the car while driving. It might've cost me the election, except the guy running against me had problems with a lawsuit tied to a shady construction deal. Let's just say I've been no angel when it comes to drinking. But in this particular instance, if the good Lord himself had been behind the wheel, the exact same thing would've occurred."

The tic shot up his left cheek, jerking like a strike on fishing line. Watkins said, "Do you have any idea how much money this could be worth to people who've been after my hide for years? Think about it. Think about it real hard, son. Two drinks don't make me tipsy enough to run over somebody."

The light inside the house seemed to warm the whole room. It had a cozy, faintly greenish hue. I looked out to towering redwoods. Between their thick trunks flashed glimpses of the sea. The senator made me edgy. I've a low tolerance level for people's self-serving bullshit. I despise my own the most.

I chose words carefully. "Sir, there's no question lots of people are going to celebrate your... situation. And I'm not saying Clint won't do everything he can to retrace every minute of Joe Garston's movements last night. And before last night. But for the moment, I'd like to suggest what I can do best is keep things relatively calm around here. Keep the media away till staff arrives. You need some quiet hours."

Watkins' face flashed red like a stoplight. "You're not getting the point. I'm telling you, nothing was there. I look at the ocean for a second. Like a couple seconds. I look back and this *body's* out in the road. Kind of crouched over. I mean, this does not look like an accident."

"We'll find out, Senator. You can be sure of it."

Watkins sprang from the couch and crossed the open living room to the kitchen. He opened a cupboard, took out a green bottle, Tanqueray gin, poured three inches into his glass. At the refrigerator he fiddled with the ice dispenser. He spoke loudly. "Hell, there's all kinds of people who'd like nothing more than to see me lose in November. For God's sake, there are people who'd rather see me dead than get another term. You'll have to wake up to that, if you're going to get to the bottom of what really happened. Do you understand what I'm telling you?"

13

I let this go unanswered. Watkins returned to the living room stirring his drink with a finger. Once on the couch, he looked to the wood ceiling and drank. Then he exhaled, saying, "Jesus Christ."

Marci came back into the room. Her face was lightly made up, her hair combed out. Little gray waves showed where it had been braided. She scooped up Allan's glass and emptied it in the kitchen sink.

Watkins gave me a sheepish, surprisingly boyish, grin.

Marci headed for the door. "Bye, Honey. Goodbye, Jeff. The Cal game's on at one. Ross Anderson's son is Cal's field goal kicker. Email Ross and Emily after. They'll remember it, come contribution time."

Marci left. Watkins tossed me the boyish grin. It was bizarre, this goofy expression on the deeply lined and wine-red face. I didn't appreciate it and so gazed out at redwood trees that swayed peacefully. As soon as the rental car started outside, Watkins went to the refrigerator and extracted two bottles of Samuel Adams beer. He popped off the caps, walked to the living room, gripping a bottle in each hand. He gave one to me, sat with the other.

Watkins had a swallow. "These'll last longer."

The beer seemed to act as fuel. After two long pulls his face grew rosier, his eyes relaxed yet alert. He reached under the coffee table, where there was a shelf for magazines. The shelf was packed with legislative paperwork. Watkins slipped out a pad of yellow, legal-sized paper. "I want you to go back and check out where it happened. I wasn't in any shape to do it right this morning. The police might've missed something. Also, find the cop who arrested me. His name's Kolatch. K-O-L-A-T-C-H. Talk to him, see what you think. He seemed off, like his mind was elsewhere. Maybe—wait, wait a minute, before I forget."

Watkins pulled out his wallet and extracted ten fifty-dollar bills. He slid the greenbacks to the middle of the coffee table. Watkins began writing on the yellow pad.

I looked at the money. "Senator, this is between you and Clint." I knew I'd take the money.

Watkins said, "I've got to pay you for what I'm asking."

I joked, "When the bill comes, you'll wish you had these."

Watkins ignored this and wrote a few more lines. "You're to have this on the side. It's our personal arrangement." He tore a page from the pad. "One last thing."

Watkins stood. The page was in his hand. "After you check out where it happened, I want you to go north till you see the sign for Garston Ranch Road. You passed it coming here. The Garstons used to be big players on the coast, but I think things have sort of fallen apart for 'em. You just never hear the name anymore." Watkins turned and headed for the hall Marci had gone down earlier. "Back in a second."

I tried to think of ways to stall until Marci returned. That way the senator wouldn't be alone with gin. I stayed seated when he came back. He put the note, now sealed in an envelope, on the coffee table.

Watkins said, "I want you to knock on their door. Give this to whoever answers. Tell them I'm devastated by their loss, then excuse yourself. Don't say or do anything else. I'm devastated by their loss. Got it?" He stacked fifty-dollar bills on top of the envelope. He lifted the beer bottle and downed a slug. "Go on. Thanks a million."

I endured the senator's agitated stare. I wanted to say I didn't have the stomach to deliver an insincere message at a time of family tragedy. I wanted to say passing on condolences was beyond the purview of my duties. I said neither. When working for Clint Sherman, nothing was beyond the sphere of your obligation. Plus I simply wanted out of that house. Let the senator be alone, no matter the consequences. If he got stinking drunk, it'd be his problem. Besides, he didn't have a car to go out in and hit somebody else.

His cell jingled. Watkins hurried to the dining room table. His heavy frame swayed with each step. He shouted into the receiver: "P.K.! Hello! Glad you got the message." He took reading glasses from the table and slid them up the rosy nose. He thumbed through papers. That Watkins was feeling better showed on his face. He said,

"You find a relevant decision yet? We'll beat the bastards on this one. You'll see. Hey, hold on."

Watkins looked at me from across the house. He pressed the phone against his stomach. The gravelly voice bellowed, "Get going, son. I'm not going to drink myself to death. I've got too many bases to cover before this thing hits the fan."

*   *   *   *

At the highway, I waited for a break in the holiday traffic. I decided to deliver the senator's note, do my duties until backup arrived, but no way in hell was I telling anybody Watkins was devastated. I turned left. A couple miles later I passed a wooden sign marked with *Garston Ranch Road* in half-chipped-away white letters. When I reached the accident site, I parked on the ocean side of the road.

I felt none of the detached professionalism I imagined Clint's veteran investigators did while working a case. I was sick in my gut looking at the blood stains that ran the direction Joe Garston was pitched by the Senator's Thunderbird. Did Joe Garston have an instant of utter shock and fear when seeing headlights come at him? Or did everything slow in his mind, and in painfully sluggish last seconds he knew he was about to get hit? Did Joe even see it coming?

I walked the shoulder of the road, looking for anything not covered by dust, a button, a comb, a scrap of cloth, which would indicate it had recently arrived, and found nothing but an empty sixteen-ounce Budweiser can. I heard a car coming and darted up the hillside for safety. A blue Ford Escort wagon, two mountain bikes preening on roof racks, whizzed by. The hill was steep. Above, where the grass ended, was a wall of ceanothus and thistle. In my head I heard Watkins: "He came out of nowhere!"

I shoved my way up through the dry brush. It crackled; leaves stuck to my clothes. I reached a knoll and swatted my shirt clean. To my surprise a dirt road was up there, paralleling the coast highway.

Beyond the road, more dry grass, then redwoods. A car passed below. Turning around, I couldn't see where I'd pushed through the brush. The thicket had sprung back. Through the thicket came the whine of another engine.

Several sets of tire tracks mingled with footprints. I duck-walked the edge of the dirt road, looking for anything unusual. I found footprints that faced each other. About a dozen formed almost a circle. One set had deep square heels, with tapered toes. Others were uneven and became lines of smudged dirt as though the person in those shoes were pushed or even dragged to the low grass on the ocean side of the terraced road.

I imagined two people fighting in the middle of night. A knee slammed a groin. They both sank, though a scruffy guy with long hair sank lower than the other. The man with the advantage grabbed the front of Joe Garston's shirt. They were spinning. Garston was flung off the dirt road, downward into brush. His hands went out. He broke through the thicket, stumbled. The earth disappeared from under him and he fell into blackness.

The imagined figure of Joe Garston was alarmingly detailed. Slight of build, average in height, he sported a greasy denim jacket worn to white in spots, jeans and motorcycle boots. His face, outlined by the long dark hair, was shiny with drink. Without thinking to do it, my hands shot forward and I dropped through the thick brush. I got going so fast I couldn't stop. Dark pavement jumped at my face in bouncing flickers. I pitched forward like a drunk Joe Garston would have. My hands scraped the roadway. Asphalt burned my palms and I tasted dust.

A horn shrieked. I ran for my life, the horn seemingly in pursuit. I fell against my car. Behind me sounded *whoosh-whoosh-whoosh*, three cars in succession. I looked up. Sunlight bounced off the ocean and struck me in blinding flashes.

"Get a grip." It was my voice, but the words seemed to come from somewhere outside of myself I couldn't trace. In those seconds while

17

falling, my brain had rocketed from the fight I'd watched in my head to my mom and the father I'd never seen. Again I heard my voice: "Get it done and get out of here."

I made a U-turn in my Jetta and drove to Garston Ranch Road. Cracked asphalt led uphill. After a tunnel of tree limbs, I passed low fences that hugged rolling pasture. The fences, made of thin upright stakes rotted by decades of rain and mist, were coated with moss and orange lichen.

At the ridge, facing the Pacific Ocean a mile away, sat an old white farmhouse. Six columns supported a wide front porch. A brick chimney, not quite straight, poked through the second story roof. There was an upstairs veranda without furniture. To the right, before a resumption of forest, were a carriage house with a black rooster weathervane, a cabin with an oversized pickup truck and rusted farm equipment out front, two tilting sheds, and a moss-covered pump house. The road approached the outbuildings before curving back to the main residence.

A Ford half-ton pickup truck was out front. It looked like it had once been silver. I parked next to it.

Walking to the house I saw bloodstains, as if they were floating on the air in front of me. I climbed a few wood stairs. Lights shone through pale-blue curtains. Before I could knock on the door, it swung inward. A tall woman with a serious face framed by dark hair stared at me as though she wasn't sure what species I was. Slender, wiry, her eyes were brown and somewhat dilated. My sliced right hand slid into a pocket of my jeans.

"If you're looking for work," she said, "there isn't any." The woman's voice—I placed her at from thirty-five to forty—was low and left no room for questions. "If you'd work a slash crew, you might try Rodota, above Comptche. He's got a deadline to meet with the Feds."

I cleared my throat. "I'm here regarding Joseph Garston. I was asked to—"

"—We already know." She did not blink or look away.

"Yes, of course. I'm very sorry. But I'd like to speak with someone regarding what happened."

She opened the door all the way and pointed to a black telephone on a table in the entry hall. "If you're from the newspapers, I've got nothing to say." She walked to the phone and picked up the receiver. "It's your choice. Leave now, or I'll have my caretaker throw you off the ranch."

"Ma'am." Even though she was only about a dozen years older than me, the occasion seemed to demand a certain formality. "My name is Jeff Taylor. I've come from Sacramento because of what happened. Senator Allan Watkins asked me, at this, this *tragedy*, to give the family his regrets." The woman did not move. I kept expecting someone to come out of a wing of the house and start an argument. I said, "I was with the senator about an hour ago." I tried to think of something true I could say. "He's a mess."

Very deliberately, she set down the telephone receiver. Every part of her grew taut. She pulled matches and a crunched pack of Camels from a back pocket of snug Levi's. She extracted a cigarette, placed it between her lips. The cellophane around the pack crinkled as she stuffed the pack back into her jeans. She lit the cigarette. Puffing it seemed to help her keep from crying, which I took to be the goal.

She whispered, "Your senator killed my little brother."

I stepped over the threshold, entering the house. "I think we should talk about it.

The tall woman looked at me as though I were crazy. She wandered off under a wooden archway on one side of the hall, her left hand holding the top of her head as if to stop it from tumbling off her neck. I heard her inhale smoke and blow it out.

She said, "So you came here to talk about it? That's very considerate of you city bastards."

I took in massive beams, and oiled knotty pine paneling the color of honey. Following her voice I came to a large room packed with furniture of the kind you see in country-town antique shops, and dark, shabby, oriental rugs. I touched the archway, hesitating beneath it. The house smelled old and complicated. She was sitting on a faded maroon divan.

She said, "I'm Kate Garston," and motioned for me to sit.

I did, in one of two faintly pink worn Tudor chairs. Kate Garston lost her battle and cried some. I looked away from her, so she would feel less uncomfortable. Oil paintings framed in dark wood lined a wall, ranch scenes and a broad seascape. Above, hanging on heavy-duty chain, was an iron-rimmed wagon wheel converted into a chandelier. The wagon wheel appeared old enough to have logged frontier miles. The windows gave view to the slowly heaving Pacific, and a lighthouse at the tip of Point Sunset. No houses or buildings intruded on the view between that parlor and the sea.

Kate patted smooth a dark, button-down shirt tucked into the snug jeans. "God," she said, and caught a breath. "You hear about these things happening to other people. You tell yourself it could've just as easily been you. Then it happens, and it doesn't seem possible it's you and not someone else anymore."

Kate puffed, and shuddered. She stared at a set of yellow porcelain teacups arranged on an end table next to the couch. Each cup had a protruding duck head at the rim, and a curly yellow tail for its handle.

She whispered, "I'm a little teapot," and tapped ashes into one of the yellow cups.

"Pardon me?" Her words had come out singsong, like a nursery rhyme. Pretty sure I'd heard her correctly, I wondered if Kate Garston were high on pot. It would explain the dilated look of her eyes. To break the heavy silence, I said, "I'm sorry. I'm very, very sorry."

She looked up, regarded me through bleary eyes. "Is this what you do? You go around and tell people you're sorry?"

"Senator Watkins is a close friend of my boss. I work for what people call a detective agency, though I'm mostly not a detective. I help out where needed."

Kate smoked, sniffed, and seemed to think this over. She shook out her brown hair. "My father used to know Allan Watkins. When Dad was president of CAWP—California Association of Wood Producers—he used to go to Sacramento about once a month. I bet there's even old programs and stuff in the filing cabinets, where they would've been at the same event."

This bit of history seemed to strike Kate Garston as important. She paused, drawing in smoke.

With the burning cigarette, Kate gestured toward the window. "When I was a kid, we used to run up to three thousand head of sheep down there. Far as you could see would be these white dabs. I used to play a game with Grandpa. When he'd get up, I'd tell him I counted them, and make up some big number, like, two thousand eight hundred and seven."

Kate looked out the window. I did the same. I saw rotting low fences missing boards here and there.

Kate said, "Grandpa'd pretend he was counting by tapping the window. He'd mumble a bunch of numbers." Her voice turned scratchy, imitating that of an old man's. "Then he'd say, 'You missed one, Katydid.'"

She looked down at the cigarette, tapped ashes into a teacup. "I used to think that was the funniest thing." Smoke drifted past her sullen face. "You'll have to excuse me, Mr. ..."

"Taylor. Jeff Taylor."

"That's right, Taylor. I know I'm not making much sense. I'm still having trouble believing it happened."

Her eyes squinted against smoke, making crow's feet at their corners. The brown hair curled inward at its tips, touching the sides of her neck. The nose was long, straight, rather aristocratic.

Kate Garston said, "Sheriff Niles told me Watkins had been drinking. My brother Joe drank like a fish himself. I'm sure that's why he was walking home. He'd lost his license for drunk driving. If he got caught driving without one again, he was going to jail."

She was gaining control over her emotions. She took a drag off her Camel, then ground it out in a teacup. "Could you tell me something?" Kate stared at me like she'd stared at other objects in the room.

"Okay."

"Can you tell me what's happening to the world? So many people nowadays spend their lives getting drunk or stoned. Those with money or position, like Allan Watkins, seem determined to piss it away. Things that took generations to build. My own mother lives in Palm Springs with a bunch of has-been TV actors and crusty stockbrokers. They look like lizards, but they think they're in hog heaven because they got a guard house and get their groceries delivered. Their lives are like fake flowers. Do you know what I mean?"

I knew precisely what she meant, but didn't offer a comment. Mainly, I was becoming interested in the death of Joe Garston. I said, "I respect what you're saying about the senator's having been drinking. Still, he passed a sobriety test at the scene."

"That's right. Then he failed the blood test when they took him in. The point is, he was drinking and driving. At two in the morning. That's not what we should get from the leaders of our state."

"I agree with you. But I'm here not only to make a feeble apology for Watkins. I had a look around at the scene of the accident. I have to tell you, I think there's a possibility foul play was involved."

Kate's legs snapped straight, pushing here to her feet.

"Foul play? You use the word *play* in connection with my brother's death?" Kate threw off a spooky, virulent light.

I stood and met her charged stare. "That was the wrong word to use. As I said, this isn't my usual type of assignment. I don't really know how to go about it."

We looked away from each other, breaking the stare-down. Cigarette smoke settled into corners of the gloomy parlor.

I said, "Is it possible there's someone who wouldn't be disappointed if your brother fell in front of a moving vehicle?"

Kate's brown eyes flared, showing whites. She stepped forward and pushed me with both hands. "You and your son of a bitching senator. I thought you were here out of some sense of decency."

"I'm just being honest. I'm wondering if Joe had any serious enemies."

Kate Garston shoved me again. "Don't you try to twist this around. Don't you dare. Get out. Get out now."

I could have sat on a faded chair and gazed out the window. Let her call the caretaker she mentioned and see if he seemed to know anything. I didn't, because under her stoic surface Kate was clearly distraught. She deserved her privacy and I'd already violated it.

Kate marched me down the hall.

At the doorway, I gave it a final shot. "If Watkins is guilty, he'll pay for it the rest of his life. But from what I've seen, you could be dealing with more than semi-drunk driving."

Kate motioned me out and shut the door. I stood on the covered porch. I'd had Kate talking and I blew it. Now I didn't know what to do. This guy Garston might have been so detested by local authorities that combined with the political juice inevitably coming with Senator Watkins, his death could bring less than a full inquiry. Easier for everyone that way. To me, this would make it seem as if a person's life held no value. At times I'd feared that about my own life. Like when Mom left, and I was alone until going off to college. Like during the weeks I spoke to no one after the hand mutilation. Or when doing a sleazy task for Sherman Investigations. If Joe Garston's life held no value, did mine? And if ours didn't, did anybody's?

I took the senator's letter from a back pocket of my jeans, set it against the wood door and headed for my car. I looked back. The whole place was still, not even a mutt digging in the weedy flower bed. Wicker chairs on the porch were littered with flaking paint. They looked as though no one had sat in them all summer, or the summer before.

Three

B ack to home base at Greenwood. It was five o'clock. I called Clint
Sherman, told him I'd rented a cabin, recounted my visit with
Allan and Marci Watkins, told him about being given five hundred
dollars and then asked to deliver a letter to the Garston family. I
described the dirt road paralleling the highway, and the footprints
directly above where Joe Garston was hit. I did not mention my
foolish plunge downhill through brush to the pavement.

Clint's froggy voice said, "Well, at least he had the sense not to go
to the Garston home himself. What happened?"

"The dead guy's sister answered the door. I gave her the senator's
note, said he was devastated, and left it at that."

The sun had lost its power. Thread-like clouds blew toward the
coast. I stood looking out the window, drifting in numb bemusement.
I'd lied about my actions, but I didn't feel guilty about omitting my
conversation with Kate Garston. I knew this meant I was finalizing
my break from Clint. The good son was rebelling. I was going to look
into Joe Garston's death without thought of protecting Clint's old
friend in any way. Senator Watkins' attitude, and his actions, propelled
me toward independence.

Clint said, "Tom Marquardt will be on the first plane from
Seattle Monday morning. Just talked to him. Now listen. I'm having
Paul Raymer and Bob Pereira drive Marquardt over on Monday.
Tell them everything you told me. Until then, keep tabs on Allan

without it being obvious what you're up to. Check in off and on, okay?"

The Cove was a restaurant and a tourist saloon at the end of a narrow lane that wound around a hill and dropped to the sea. Two dozen cars formed a neat row near the back wall of the faded red building. I noted a scarcity of pickup trucks, unusual for the region.

Inside the bar, nicely dressed couples sipped drinks in front of a river rock fireplace. Their chatter blended into the aggregate hum of people on holiday. I went to a stool covered with shiny red vinyl at the far end of the bar. At the other end, where the counter curved to meet the wall, two guys in white shirts and dark ties meticulously loosened around their collars hooted over a game of Liar's Dice.

The bartender was a short stocky man with an oiled flattop haircut. His hands moved quickly, drying glasses as though working against a clock.

"What'll it be?" His hands didn't cease moving.

"A Heineken sounds perfect."

The bartender ran a towel in a circle on the counter, set down my beer and a frosted mug. He went back to drying glasses and setting them in rows. I had a swallow and commented upon the beauty of the area. The bartender asked if this was my first visit to Sunset County. I said I'd driven through over the years, but only stopped for gas or snacks.

I added, "I should tell you I'm investigating the death of Joe Garston."

The man nodded, dried glasses. Dice rattled on the bar. "Does the sheriff know about you?"

"I posted Senator Watkins' bail this morning." I took a swallow of beer. "It's no secret I'm up here."

The bartender's face stretched tight. His lower lip protruded in a kind of fish-lips pout. "You know, some guy has a few pops and kills himself on these bad roads, I can be found liable. The family can claim I pushed drinks on him." He shook his head. "That's the law nowadays. You got to be your customer's keeper, or you can lose everything."

"So you're saying Senator Watkins wasn't drunk when he left here."

"I didn't push no drinks on him. I got witnesses."

"I believe you." Sapphire light flashed in the doorway, and a party of four came in. The bartender nodded at them. I put a fifty-dollar bill on the counter. The bartender pocketed the fifty without missing a beat in drying and setting glasses in well-ordered rows. Purely for entertainment, I dropped another fifty on the counter. The bill disappeared. It was like feeding fresh mackerel to a seal.

I said, "I'm interested in what you saw last night. Anything you can remember might help."

"Well, he came in a little past midnight. I've served him over the years. Big tipper. Always friendly, but he lets you know to keep a distance. More like old-time stature than these slick guys from tech. He wasn't slick."

I nodded. Watkins would never be perceived as slick. That was the one thing I appreciated about him.

Dice hit the counter. People talked. The bartender pointed to a small window table.

"He sat over there, looking through a bunch a papers." A round wooden table faced rocking purple waves. "He came to the bar for his drinks. We don't got waitress service after twelve. Your man drank G and Ts. Three of them."

"You sure it wasn't two?"

The bartender shot me a look designed to show how stupid the question was. "How about if I tell you once more? I could lose my business over an extra martini. Your senator put down two G and Ts so fast I decided to keep an eye on him. It was late, the man looked tired. I made the third one as weak as I could get away with."

An older, dapper couple waltzed in. In an animated chorus, they called "Hal!" and ordered drinks before reaching the bar. I left, passing through a lobby to the restaurant. I put my name in for a table. Back in the bar, the place was filling up. A blond-haired man, pretending his right fist was a microphone, sang with the jukebox, vowing eternal devotion to his love. I re-took my place at the far end of the counter, finished the beer and asked for another.

Hal nodded, brought it. Speaking lower than before, he said, "Between you and me and the wall, I hate to see a man ruin himself over a twerp like Garston. The kid's born into local royalty, and he's no damn good. That brat was lucky to last as long as he did."

"Is that so?"

Hal rose a hand. "Got it." He went down the bar, to where the waitress had set a tray. He mixed two drinks. A 1980s rock song playing on the jukebox ended and was followed by another '80s hit. A roll of laughter came from the swelling group sitting near the unlit fireplace.

When Hal came back, he grabbed an ice pick. His hairy arm rose and fell into an open metal cooler.

I said, "You're the third person I've talked to about Joe. The other two said the same thing. That he did a lot of drinking."

"That and everything else. I say that because of who you'd see him with."

"Was he in here last night?"

"Nope. The young folks around here hang out at Art's. It's kind of a pizza and beer joint back in town. They only got a beer and wine license, but that's what most kids drink today. Besides, they'll look the other way over there if you partake in a little something extra in the restroom."

Hal hustled down the bar to pour a drink. Watching him, I saw the high school girl who was the restaurant hostess poke her head into the room. She caught my eye and waved a red menu. I recognized her. My heart jumped.

Then I realized I'd never seen her before in my life.

The waitress led me to an intimate corner table, the same kind of table Watkins sat at in the bar the night before. I watched the same purple ocean the Senator had. Outside, the world grew darker.

I ordered a third Heineken and checked out the menu. I couldn't settle down. I'd never felt emotionally involved in any of the assignments I'd handled for Sherman Investigations. If someone needed a man to escort his secretary/secret girlfriend to a company function; if someone needed to be talked up on the golf course to relay a potential compromise in a business deal, or deliver a polite threat; if someone needed to be informed it was in his best interest to forget something he had seen or heard—that was my job. I'd never once felt a connection to the outcome. Now, Joe Garston's death, the senator's carrying on, plus emotions I couldn't identify, were changing that.

I ate sea trout. I was tired, and tipsy. I looked around and wondered what it had been like for Watkins in the bar. I figured he was lost in his paperwork and hadn't noticed much about his surroundings.

I paid for dinner with another of the senator's fifties, and walked into purple night. To the east, the ridge rose like a black stripe paralleling the coastline. Amidst clouds, I made out a rising moon. I got in my car and headed up the narrow road that led to the highway. I was going to Art's, the pizza and beer place. Maybe the bartender there would be as chatty as Hal.

Behind me, headlights swung onto the road.

There hadn't been voices in the parking lot, or noises of car doors opening or shutting. The headlights followed closely. Using the side mirror, on turns I saw a jacked-up pickup truck. I snapped on the left blinker. Without coming to a stop I turned right. If I was going to have to confront somebody, it would be smarter to keep it away from Sunset, away from the locals at Art's. The gravel road to the studio cabin I'd rented was perfect. If I had to get physical, I wanted to be as discreet as possible.

At least I'd learned something: Kate Garston probably had a husband or a boyfriend. I hadn't had the opportunity to piss off anyone else. It also occurred to me I had no idea what was in the senator's letter I'd delivered. Considering his state of mind, it could have been ludicrous enough to send a loved one over the edge. The mile to Greenwood rolled by. The beers had given me a pleasant buzz. The headlights followed at an unchanging distance.

I turned off the highway, bounced along gravel past a few cabins. The pickup followed. Ahead was a vast blankness, sea and night sky. I parked. The truck's lights blinked off. Not looking behind me, I got out of my car. A door to the pickup opened with the groan of pinched metal. It slammed shut so hard I heard a rattling of the truck's frame. I started toward the cabin.

A voice bellowed, "Hey asshole, ain't you curious?"

I was curious enough to walk slower, and curious enough to stop walking altogether as footsteps moved over gravel.

I spun and faced a shadowy mass that bounded forward like some kind of monster from the deep. That he was as tall as I am, six-three, and much wider, did not trouble me. And nothing shined, no knife, no gun, no pipe wrench.

The man stopped ten feet away. "I want to talk to you."

I brought my hands up. "Not a problem." I'd developed a method of turning my right hand into a kind of hook I used to collar someone while I punched with my left. I said, "Talk to me." I estimated the dark monster weighed two hundred and seventy pounds.

The man breathed as though he had run a long way. He said, "You know, you're a real ass—"

A fist sailed, a genuine haymaker. I ducked under it and charged. My forehead struck his chest. I drove him against the door of my Jetta. I heard the door *thump* back in a dent. Wind shot out of him. The car rocked like a boat. He was too big for me to waste time with diplomacy; I punched with my good hand, solidly to the kidneys, three fast blows. The man grunted. I hooked with another left to the stomach, but he didn't bend over more than a couple of inches as I backed away. I hooked again, hitting the shadowy monster on the chest rather than his chin. My knuckles hit his coat, his fleshy

29

thickness. They did not strike bone. I reached for him with my pincer of a right hand, to pull him downward and get in a better punch.

The guy's fist struck the side of my head like a club. I buckled, throwing another left hook into air. His second blow to my head sent me to the ground so fast I don't remember the trip. A boot tore across my gut. My head felt like it had been pumped full of air, then split with a hatchet. Rolling across gravel, I popped up. The hurt would go away. It always did. The guy started circling, grunting and cursing. My feet, shuffling over loose pebbles, mirrored the monstrous silhouette's wider arc. My vision was bad. I couldn't get a fix on the attacker.

I took in as much air as I could, to replenish the leaking in my head. "What do you want?"

"Hey, pal, I ask the questions." A steamy exhale blasted like exhaust. Head jerking forward and back, he threatened with short jabs of both arms. "I want to know what you were doin' today, up at the Garstons."

"The person who hit Joe asked me to relay his sympathies."

"Bullshit. She was handlin' it okay, then you fed her some bullshit!"

I decided to make a run for it. Lose the big bastard in the sand dunes and make a big circle back to see if he drove off. My feet pushed off gravel. So did his, and the man's arms were just long enough and just strong enough to make a flying tackle. He wrenched me sideways. I kicked him hard. This had no effect. He wrapped his arms tight around my middle. He hoisted me into the cold damp night air; a moment later I bounced off gravel.

My mouth burned from scraping rock. I got up to fight. Everything was muffled, wavy. I spit blood and a few pebbles. My arms seemed made of straw. I went to hit him. The man simply stepped forward, grabbed the front of my shirt, and firmly sat me down.

He said, "You goddamn stay away from the Garstons. Hear me? You bother Kate again, it'll be worse."

The man disappeared into fuzzy, quaking darkness. His truck

started, gravel flew behind spinning tires. Headlights blinked on. The outsized pickup truck carrying an outsized man roared off.

Flat on my back, there seemed to be a lot of fog between me and the moon. A lot of fog in my ears, too. My tongue cleaned away debris I spit out. It came upon a couple of uneven edges in my top teeth.

I listened to the call of the sea. I tasted blood. A car passed by out on the highway. As far as I could tell, life was undisturbed at the other cabins. I was glad for that. I preferred to grovel alone on the blue shale. I preferred trying to remember if the boot that stomped me had a tapered point, like some of the footprints above the accident site. But I hadn't a guess. I hadn't been fleet enough of foot to elude Kate Garston's protector, nor had I possessed the presence of mind to try to check out his Sasquatch-sized boots.

Four

First thing Sunday morning, I called Clint Sherman and recounted what had happened the night before. Clint suggested I take photos in case documentation was later needed. At ten o'clock I was sitting in a cozy bakery with the county sheriff. Outside, silvery light split through fog in expanding beams, promising full sun by noon. Tourists in colorful clothing bought newspapers and checked out real estate ads taped to office windows. Low-slung foreign cars lined the sidewalks.

Sheriff Niles was in street clothes, a tent-like blue pullover shirt and jeans. A corpulent man of forty-odd years, his legs were too short for the rest of him. His tidy clipped hair was neither light nor dark. His face resembled a medicine ball made of uncooked oatmeal. We both had a cup of hot coffee at hand. On the platter between us was a stack of four apple fritters, each nearly as large as a dinner plate. Niles seemed to examine the goodies individually, as though they were specimens of rare beauty.

He placed a fritter on a paper plate and slid it at me. He said, "Yes?"

Niles grabbed one and tore two bites without chewing. His mouth full, he said, "If you want to know what I can tell you about the Garston case, partake in table with me."

I sipped steaming coffee. It burned my sore lips. "I'll partake," I said. "It's the pace I'll have trouble with."

Niles laughed and killed the fritter. His stomach bumped the table, coffee splashed. "You're the first private eye I ever met who doesn't act like he's on TV. You haven't even flashed me your badge. They always smile when they show me their badge."

To endear myself to the sheriff, I bit off a large chunk of sticky pastry and spoke with my mouth full. "Okay. Let's start with whether you know of any strangers hanging around Art's pizza. Someone who could've taken Joe Garston and dumped him in front of the senator's car."

Niles attacked his second fritter, swallowed. He said, "Town's full of strangers all summer. You're a stranger. But to answer the question, no. Joe left Art's a little before one o'clock. He walked out without saying anything. But he was like that. He'd get soused, and about the time he might pass out he'd head home. He was like a friggin' salmon. Something always told Joe when to head upstream. Until yesterday, he always made it back to the ranch."

"He lived up there?"

"Who else would have him?"

"I see," I said, though so far all I saw was that Joe Garston was a drunk who had been killed by a drunk. "Have you climbed the hill at the scene of the accident?"

Niles nodded, and grunted through another mouthful of pastry. "I climbed it. Didn't find nothin'."

I set the coffee down and leaned toward the beefy sheriff. "C'mon, you saw the footprints and tire tracks on the road above from where Watkins says Joe appeared out of nowhere. They have to make you wonder. You can't just ignore what he claims happened. Watkins passed the sobriety test at the scene."

"He failed a blood test about twenty minutes later."

"I'm just saying he was lucid."

Niles bounced on the caned webbing of his chair. I found it impossible to dislike him. Heavy eyelids blinking, he said, "Hell, Taylor, I said I found nothing on the *hill*side. Up there on the logging road, most of them truck tracks are mine. I was on that road at sunrise. Damn cold out there, too."

The jiggles subsided; he had a swallow of coffee. "Look, if you go south on that road half a mile, you reach Garston Creek. There's a swimmin' hole where kids go. Anybody local who wants to fish a cove along there, they won't park next to the highway. It's too dangerous. I guess Joe proved that. They park on the old logging road and walk down to the ocean. Kate Garston leaves that road open as a courtesy."

"That's Garston property above where he got hit?"

"Yep. Basically it's a fire break, but the Garstons have been letting people use it since her great-granddaddy cut it himself."

I ventured another bite of apple fritter. "Still, what about the footprints? Directly above where Garston was hit there's a cluster of footprints. Kind of in a circle. They look like they head into the grass. You see those?"

The round oatmeal face nodded. "Photographed them and took soil samples. At the moment they're a few more footprints among hundreds. Just people going out to catch some rock cod. You like to fish? God's greatest gift to the common man."

"I did when I was a kid. I haven't fished for years."

Niles covered one eye. It made him look like he was peeking as he nodded toward my mangled hand and said, "None of my business, but you get that on the job?"

"In a way I did."

"What way might that be?"

I couldn't help messing with him. I lied. "When we settled out of court, I had to sign a non-disclosure agreement. They can come after me if I talk about what happened. Let's just say I didn't get the worst of it."

Niles let out a low whistle. He shook his head, uncovered his eye. He finished his second apple fritter and carefully set about wiping his mouth with paper napkins.

I took up the coffee and looked around the crisply lighted pastry shop. At half a dozen tables people read thick Sunday papers from San Francisco and Sacramento. Their self-satisfied airs were alien to me. I had not the slightest idea how to take comfort in food, newspapers and morning coffee.

I said, "I don't expect you to listen to me, but the Senator, the only witness, swears he looked at the ocean for a couple seconds, turned back and Garston was in the middle of the road. He said, 'He came out of nowhere.' I can't forget those words. I hope you won't forget them, either."

Niles backed his gut off the edge of the table. "I won't. I'm confident you, Watkins and that asshole press aide of his who called me this morning won't, either. Quit the speech-making and I'll level with you. I got five deputies and twenty-four hours a day, seven days a week, to watch over a stretch of highway north to Westly, south to Ross Cove, and inland to near Anderson Valley. Can you dig it? That don't even include handling dog bites. You being here is to my liking. You seem to have the time, and the inclination, to find out if there's anything suspicious. Yes? No?"

He snatched a third fritter, took a bite. Sugary apple filling oozed out one side of his mouth. "Ask whatever questions you want. If I can, I'll answer them."

"Fine. The senator appreciates your cooperation." I drank some coffee. I was reciting the proper lines, but I wasn't sure who I was speaking for. Allan Watkins? Clint Sherman? Myself?

I said, "Maybe you can identity somebody for me." I told Niles about being followed to Greenwood, and the fight.

Niles took a bite of pastry and massaged his cheeks as he chewed. "Oh boy, you mean B-B. Bobby Stiving. Bobby the Bear." He spoke through food and kneading fingers. "He was raised on the Garston place. His parents were caretakers in the old days, and he's stayed on doing chores and running a log choker for her." The sheriff swallowed. He crinkled his nose. "Why didn't you run?"

"I did, but he made a hell of a tackle."

Sheriff Niles pushed the last chunk of sticky pastry down his gullet. He said, "I seen you been whomped. I just didn't want to say anything, on account of, you know, your hand. It'd be like rubbing it in." This time he wiped both hands on the opposite sleeves of his tent shirt. "You should've been faster. You're a pretty big kid, but B-B made it to state finals in wrestling. Got a full ride down to UCLA, but he couldn't handle life in the city. Got in a hell of trouble—hey, I don't like it. Kate's got that man trained like a bird dog."

I had a sip of coffee, touched my tongue to a bump on my upper lip. "Are she and Stiving lovers?"

Niles ignored the question. He pushed further away from the table, and stood. He didn't rise much. "Come with me, brother."

Niles waved to the locals as we left Connie's Home Baked. They smiled and tipped their baseball caps. We walked along Main Street.

I said, "You know, this Kate Garston, it's hard to get a sense of what she's like. I talked to her for a fair amount of time, but, uh, I came away not sure if she's all there or not. What's her story?"

Niles clamped a hand on my arm. He smelled of hot coffee and sweets. "Don't ask me to gossip like that. I won't do it."

He stepped off the sidewalk and opened the passenger door of an old lime-green gas guzzler, a Bonneville from the early 2000s. Bending over to reach the glove box, his stomach drooped onto the seat.

Niles found what he wanted, worked his wide body back out of the car and turned around. He said, "I'd like to give this here to you."

In his chubby hand was a piece of dark glass about three inches across. The glass was splintered and held together by the glued label of a Korbel brandy bottle.

Niles examined it. "I went crawling around the rocks at low tide, across the road from where Joe got smushed. That's where I found this. I think it might interest you. It's not evidence. It's just a piece of glass that was soaking wet. You can have it."

He set the dark glass in my palm.

Niles said, "Next time you and Watkins are yakkin' about us locals making life rough for him, ask him for a nightcap." Niles winked. "See what he serves."

Splinters of glued glass pricked my hand. I imagined Joe Garston's body, face down on the highway. "If I'm ever satisfied Watkins did it, I'll call you and say you were right. For now, I don't know."

"I think you would call. I got a feeling you're that kind of guy." Sheriff Niles let his bulk sag against the side of the lime Bonneville. "Go ahead, ask me anything you want."

"Kate. Is she married? Just the facts, no gossip."

Niles grinned, looked to the clearing sky. "Good-looking woman like that. I can't figure her. She won't mingle with anyone in town who arrived in this century, but at the same time she hangs out with that artsy-fartsy crowd in the hills. Anyway..." Niles rubbed his eyes. It looked like he was focusing binoculars. "There was a time, back when she was in school in Davis, when everybody said she and Eddie Lantis were engaged. Nothing ever came of it."

"The way you say his name, can I take it this Lantis was from Sunset County?"

"And is." Niles pointed through town, northeast, toward hills. "Lives forty miles that-a-way. He comes from a logging family, too." He shook his jowls some more. "It was funny. They were supposed to get married in summer, then you never saw them together anymore. Or heard what the breakup was about. Lordy, that's sixteen, no, more like twenty, yeah, like twenty years ago."

"Joe? I'm assuming he wasn't married. Nobody's mentioned a wife."

Niles's face came alive. "Now there's a story! About five years ago he just up and married Molly Wells." Saying the name Molly Wells seemed to brighten Niles' day. He bounced on his toes. "She's a Wells, as in Wells Beach, yes? Even today the old families tend to stick together. I think she and Joe didn't make it because they were too much alike."

37

I said, "How long ago did they split up? If it's not gossiping."

Niles said, "They went separate ways about two years ago."

"What's her story?"

"Go see for yourself. She's real entertainment. Lives over in Ukiah now."

"Okay, then tell me what question I didn't ask that I should have."

Niles took out his cell and checked the time. His face sank, settled. "You know what," he said, "I'm plumb pushed for time. I got to take the wife to church up in Anchor Bay. The missus don't ask much, but I was late for church once and she served me dog food for dinner three nights running. She used the same bowl Tipper usually gets, and he got my pork chops."

Niles smiled and shook his head. He waddled around the front of the car. He plopped onto the driver's seat. The vehicle sank, and rose. I saw his hand turn the key. The engine came to life. Niles backed out of the parking space, smiled like a clean-shaven Santa stuffed into civilian clothes, and drove out of town.

The tips of his boots were pointed, but he'd already said he was up on that road. I didn't think Sheriff Niles pushed Joe Garston down the hill into oncoming traffic. I did wonder what he really thought about the footprints.

Five

I walked to Sunset General Store, bought a large gray sweatshirt, a three pack of white socks, a pair of dark socks, a disposable razor and a toothbrush/toothpaste kit. I went to the little city park on a rocky headland above the ocean, and in the bathroom shaved with cold water, garnering odd looks from guys coming in to pee. I put on the sweatshirt. I went to the Chevron station for gas, then drove up the coast to the Watkins' rented hideaway. A white Mercedes was parked next to the bronze Taurus rental.

Marci Watkins answered the door. She took my hand, this time without blinking. I entered the living room. The senator stepped forward and shook my stubby hand in a manner so low key I was automatically put on guard.

Watkins introduced me to two people. One was Ruth Beldon, a thirtyish brunette whose hair was snipped around her head like an upside-down soup bowl. She wore round granny glasses and was busy at a laptop that was on the kitchen table. Eyes on glowing screen, Ruth Beldon smiled, waved, and continued typing. "This is Lee Welty," Watkins said of the man who stepped forward, nodded aggressively, and did not shake hands. "He's head of media for the campaign."

Although we'd never met, I knew of Welty. In his early thirties, he was a pollster, sometimes lobbyist, a whiz at all forms of public relations. He had on a white shirt, a blood-red tie, dark slacks and shiny black shoes. His fair hair was neatly trimmed, parted on the left. He wore ochre-tinted aviator glasses. He smiled as easily as he breathed.

Welty said, "Allan's been telling me about you." He motioned for me to sit in the black recliner.

I sat. I already didn't like Welty. His tone indicated he was about to hustle me.

Welty sat on the couch. His hands dropped between his knees in a phony one-of-the-guys pose. "Clint Sherman called the senator this morning. How's the head? We understand you took a severe beating last night."

"Unfortunately, I've had worse."

Welty pointed toward Watkins, who was at the refrigerator extracting little green bottles of Perrier. Welty said, "Allan says the attacker must have been an intimate of the Garston family. Apparently, he was trying to stop you from going about your investigation."

I turned and spoke across the cabin, to Watkins. "His name's Bobby Stiving. He's caretaker up at the ranch."

Lee Welty's eyes lit up behind the wide glasses. "We want you to go into Sunset and file assault charges." To Watkins, he said, "I'll get you something on local TV tonight. The papers tomorrow. Ruth's got social media. It looks fishy as hell, somebody attacking the person looking into this."

Allan said. "Good. Just don't overdo it."

The changes that had come over Watkins in a day were remarkable. He was so tentative I figured Welty had slapped down rules, making it clear that a misstep meant the end of the senator's career. Ironically, the Allan Watkins who the day before had been jabbering on the phone, beer in hand, plowing ahead with the work he believed in, didn't seem quite so evil anymore. He seemed human.

The senator nearly bowed as he handed out fizzy water. "Enjoy." He pulled a mahogany rocker over from near the granite fireplace.

Sweet Jesus, I thought, this twit has scared Watkins into his best behavior. I said, "I already told Sheriff Niles what happened." I touched a lump on my head, shrugged. "I didn't mention any charges, on the assumption it helps to be on good terms with the locals."

Lee Welty sat back. He smiled a glassy smile. He could have been presenting Lotto winnings or shooting a neighbor's cat. He said, "You didn't sign anything, correct?" He followed the remark with an emphatic nod.

I set down the mineral water. The messy stacks of legislative papers had been removed from the coffee table. In their place were current issues of *Field and Stream*, *The Outdoorsman* and *Back Country*. The magazines were obviously fresh off a rack. And Watkins was dressed in an earth-toned cashmere sweater, dark slacks and new-looking Rockport shoes. His silvery hair had a sculpted look that told me it had been sprayed into place. And Welty had him off the booze. The senator rubbed a thumb over the spot on his cheek where the tic sprang from.

I said, "I'm not pressing any charges. The Garstons don't need another problem in their life."

Welty stood, hitched his slacks then settled back on the couch. "Hold it right there. Let's not get heroic and skip over actual damages done to you."

"I'm not damaged. I got in a fight and lost."

Beyond the senator, who self-consciously drank water, Ruth Beldon tapped keys. Marci put a hen in the oven. She wore a long white dress that had swarms of crimson dragonflies appliquéd on it. The cabin smelled faintly of cleaning fluids.

Welty slid his cuffs. He placed the tips of his fingers together. The artificial sincerity in his voice, and the ease of his glassy smile, were phenomenal. He said, "See, Jeff, you've got to keep in mind there is a bigger picture. We're talking about Allan's position as a leader in the senate, and the way the voters perceive that leader vis-à-vis this incident. Not the specific charges, but the more general image that Allan was driving under the influence."

"Which I wasn't," Watkins added.

41

"Sir, you were drinking. The bartender at The Cove swears it was three gin and tonics, not two. And you failed the blood test when they took you in."

The senator's jaw dropped. A rarity, he was speechless.

Nothing fazed Welty. "Which is irrelevant, since he passed the roadside sobriety test. We'll show the blood test was improperly administered. They didn't know what they were doing. Look, there's plenty of room to maneuver in the courts, but only after he's found innocent in the hearts and minds of the voters."

I looked around. No one else seemed to think Lee Welty was a comedian. Or a bad joke incarnate. "Sounds like a real winner," I said. "But I don't see what it's got to do with me asking the police to go after Stiving for our fight. The guy's a life-long employee of the family. I grew up in a town like Sunset. People settle things directly, person to person."

Welty let his hands drop. "Certain interests have been trying to entrap the senator for years." He went to the kitchen area, picked up a folder from the table and recited as he opened it: "May the sixteenth, two thousand and twelve. Senator Watkins has dinner with the North Valley Water Committee at Frank Fat's. After, in the bar, a hottie approaches and claims her date left without her. She already knows Allan's name and asks for a ride to, quote, 'home or wherever.'"

Welty licked a finger and turned back sheets. "The twenty-third of December, two thousand and fifteen. Leaving a Christmas party at the Fairmont Hotel, San Francisco, the check girl hands Marci a mink coat. She says she was told it's a surprise Christmas gift. This is when the last shot at a new dam below Shasta is going in front Allan's committee in January." Welty looked up. His face was grave. "You're probably not old enough to remember, but at that point in time this was the hottest water issue in California. Allan killed the bill in committee, even though his own district would have profited from its passage. Are you beginning to see the picture? I've got a list that continues to a year ago May."

42

The senator had gone to the kitchen for more water. He called across the house. "This kind of crap has been going on since I got seniority on Ways and Means."

The expression on Welty's face made it seem something had been pushed from a gray area to black and white.

I said, "I get it. Lobbyists have been trying to buy off the senator for years. Now this thing with Joe Garston happens. I don't see any connections between that, or me getting in a fight."

Welty closed the folder. He rapped at the coffee table as if it were a bongo drum. "Not on the surface, no. In fact, there need not be any actual connections. We're talking about perceived connections in the public's mind."

In the kitchen the senator could be heard discussing food and table settings. His voice was a rumble of false interest.

I shook my head, *No*.

Lee Welty countered with vigorous nods. "The internet and the tube will blur it. The average voter is not going to separate bribes Allan has been offered, his passing a roadside sobriety test, this Garston guy being a bum, and you, a former two-time All America basketball player getting severely beaten for asking normal questions."

My voice jumped from my chest: "You're out of your mind. And I was all conference, not All America. They're not even close to the same thing."

Welty's face was expressionless. His wristwatch beeped and he glanced at it. He said, "Don't get in my way, Jeff."

Senator Watkins rushed back with more Perrier. The wrinkles on his face pulled every which way. "Gentlemen," he said, "disagreeing is fine, arguing is not." Watkins put a cold bottle in my hand. "We're all in this together."

Lee Welty said, "What I've been trying to do here, is explain some concepts to Jeff. But we don't have to get hung up on that."

Watkins sat in the mahogany rocker.

I guzzled the contents of the second bottle of mineral water. I wondered: would Clint Sherman play along with this? Or would he maybe go to the kitchen, pour himself a glass of gin and watch Welty grow nervous as the senator went haywire twitching? I hoped, though doubted, the latter.

All I could think to say was, "If Garston was set up to get hit, it seems like we should be trying to rip everything open instead of forcing things into neat little packages."

Welty was unruffled. "Jeff," he said, "we're doing a phone conference in an hour with the editors from the *Chronicle* and the *Redding Courier*. So, before Allan and I prep, fill us in on what information you have harvested so far."

"That's what I came for."

I turned to the senator. Welty cut me off before I could begin.

"We're pressed for time. We need answers. How about the victim's sister? I made some calls and learned the two of them were partners in a multi-million-dollar logging company. My sources tell me Garston was an alcoholic, and he and his sister battled about it."

I said, "The clerk I posted bail with told me basically the same thing."

Welty said, "The sister probably comes into substantial money at his death. Can I assume you've determined her whereabouts at two a.m. yesterday?"

I felt a snapping in my head that I knew well. I looked to Watkins. "I'm not going to talk to this phony piece of shit anymore. Period."

Ruth Beldon quit typing. Marci, basting brush over the roasting hen, was still. Senator Watkins practically cracked his teeth on the Perrier bottle. His need for alcohol had just soared.

Welty folded his hands, looked down and shook his head in an artificial, dippy sorrow.

I said, "I don't have to put up with this." My head spun like after Bobby Stiving had slammed me against gravel. Dizzy as I was, I got to my feet. I was going to break Lee Welty's perfect nose. Maybe choke him with his shiny red TV newscaster's tie. Choke him, then use the tie to throw him to the floor. Give the slick bastard an eye-opening experience of real life.

I moved at Welty but veered left and looped back to the door. Through clenched teeth, I said, "I'll write up a report and have it to you in the morning."

Watkins came after me. "*Son*," he said. He looked a little frightened. "The election's nine weeks from Tuesday. A young man has died. Everybody's on tight strings."

I opened the door. "Of course. But I know you're better than this, this sick joke of a human being."

Welty's folded hands flew up. He rushed past the senator. "You're fired. You're fired, Taylor. Now get out."

I pushed him hard. Welty stumbled backwards. I took half a step toward him—and knew for certain Welty wasn't worth kicking the shit out of. He wasn't worth the trouble it would bring. I looked past him to Senator Watkins, who furiously massaged the tic on his left cheek. The senator's face was the color of sand. His eyes seemed larger and grayer than before.

I said, "Am I fired?"

Watkins glanced at the green bottle in his hand. He spoke calmly. "It's just me and what I saw out there. It's going to be hard to prove I'm innocent."

He went to take a drink; the bottle of mineral water was empty. "I think—look, it might not matter what really happened, because there will always be questions. Guilty or innocent, it'll never go away."

Watkins held himself with a kind of old-man's dignity. I wanted to hate him, for selling out to Welty, and because his drinking and driving were connected, one way or another, with killing someone. But I didn't hate him, partly because he was so weak and partly because he was so strong.

Welty said, "Can't you understand English? You're fired. Be on your way."

Still I thought Watkins might come to his senses and tell Welty to back off. Instead, the senator again brought the empty bottle to his lips, then let it drop to his belly.

He said, "Lee's in charge of all aspects of media for the campaign."

I walked outside without shutting the door and tromped down the redwood stairs. I got in my dark Jetta and reversed half a circle. Looking in the rear-view mirror, I saw Allan Watkins standing at the bottom of the stairs. He'd followed me. He waved. His reflection shrunk rapidly as I drove into the shadows of ancient trees. In the senator's left hand was a small dark bottle. It wasn't Perrier.

Six

I wandered around the tiny cabin at Greenwood, cursing. Lee Welty was a walking TV set. He had the emotional and intellectual depth of a birdbath. He was part of that sea of people on the rise who don't know the difference between plastic and wood, a Twitter feed from conversation. I had bumped into people like Welty at every turn in life and they always provoked outrage.

I kept telling myself to settle down, to write out everything I'd done the previous thirty hours. I was going to have some explaining to do. With luck Clint Sherman would have occasion to meet with the living TV set. That would put me in the clear as far as getting fired, which was ironic as hell in that I had actually quit my position with Sherman Investigations less than a week before.

I couldn't settle down. The death of Joe Garston had become personal. It had slipped under the surface of events and lodged itself in that place I knew so little about, my own heart. There were currents of feelings that baited and pressed me backwards in time. Superficially, these took form when I momentarily thought the menu-waving hostess at The Cove was a girl I grew up with, as though a decade had not passed. That sense of stepping back into my past was stirred by the fresh smell of evergreens, the two-lane highway with ocean on one side, hills rising on the other, and the pinging freshness of the air. It wasn't nostalgia that stirred and confused me. The only clear thought I had was that at twenty-five, like when I was a kid, I was spending an inordinate amount of time alone.

There was knocking on the door. It was past noon, check-out hour, and I hadn't fulfilled my obligation to go to the main house and declare my intentions with regard to another night's lodging.

When I opened the door a slender figure, head hidden under the shiny blue hood of a windbreaker, dashed in. Her cheeks were flushed.

I stepped back. I said, "Hey, about yesterday. I was out of line."

Kate Garston flipped off the blue hood. "Screw that." She shut the door behind her. She unzipped and got out of the light windbreaker.

We stared at each other for a few seconds. Kate caught a breath, exhaled, caught another breath.

I said, "I didn't hear a car. It must be the wind."

"I left my truck at the old wharf and hiked up the beach."

Kate glanced at my hook hand; I slid it out of view.

"Would you care to sit down?"

I took the windbreaker from her and draped it over the back of a chair that faced the little eating table. Kate sat on the couch. I figured the wharf must have been a fair distance because her temples were damp with sweat. Her chestnut hair was frizzy at the tips.

I went to the sink, rinsed a glass, filled it with cold water and brought it to her. Kate looked out the window at the choppy ocean. I sat on the other end of the couch.

Kate sipped water. The longer the silence continued, the more interesting it became.

Kate didn't turn from looking out the window. She said, "People talk. I didn't want anybody to see me coming here."

"I understand."

Kate said, "I'm on my way to pick up my mom at the Santa Rosa airport. I wanted to talk to you first."

"I'll be glad to talk to you. But," I added, as if I didn't know, "how did you know I was here?"

She turned. She grinned wanly. "I had our caretaker find out where you're staying."

I tapped the blue swelling on my lower lip. "You know, I met your caretaker. He wasn't much for light conversation."

Her smile fell. In her preoccupation Kate hadn't noticed the purple lip or cuts on the mouth and swelling on the left side of my face. She said, "Oh, shit." She stamped the floor. What looked like anger flashed across her face, but I wasn't sure. It was not possible to read her. Kate said, "I had no idea he'd do anything like this. I'll have him apologize."

"No thanks. He might misunderstand the order."

She set the water glass on the table. She looked tired. "I only wanted to know where you were staying, so I could talk with you. I have some things I want to tell you."

I went to the bathroom and returned with a washcloth. I handed it to Kate and sat on the couch. "I can't say I know what it's like to lose a brother. I feel bad for you, and bad for him, too."

Kate used the washcloth. Sniffing, she said, "You're one of the few. Joe didn't have a whole lot of real friends." Her breathing chugged. "That's not what I came to tell you."

"Not a problem. There's no hurry."

She dried her eyes. "Okay, here goes. Last spring, Joe drove to Ukiah and withdrew twelve grand from a company account. When I came across it in a bank statement, and pressed him on it, he went crazy." She waved a hand, dismissing her last comment. "That's not the point. What I have to tell you is he never bought anything big that I saw. He used to take money about once a year, but it always turned into a boat, a motorcycle. A trip to Baja with his ex. This time, nothing."

"I'm not exactly clear on where all this money's coming from. Your logging company?"

She nodded. "I do our banking over in Ukiah, to keep the local noses from snooping into our affairs." Her red-rimmed brown eyes met mine. "Oh, that's right. You don't know about things."

"I know a bit more than nothing."

As the talk steered further from Joe, Kate patted and shaped her hair. "See, we are, were, equal owners of Garston Timber, LLC. It's what's left of what my great-grandfather started. To make a long story short, when the recession of 2008 dried up the construction market, we nearly went under. My dad got tired of fighting, and my parents sold to a corpo based in Georgia. The deal finally closed in 2014. I managed to hang onto almost a third of the land for me and Joe. It worked out better tax wise. A continuing operation gave Mom and Dad expenses to write off against profits from the sale."

Her eyes seemed to lack a point of focus. "Is this helping?"

"You've told me Joe took money from a company account. Why do I need to know that?"

She went to the picture window. She tipped her forehead against glass. "Joe hung around with people who used him because they knew he had access to money. After he took out that money last spring, I changed things so his name is only on the monthly expenses account. It's probably illegal, but anyway, about three weeks ago he tried to get money and the bank turned him down. Any account with significant assets requires my signature now. We had a hell of a fight. He threatened to sell out to a stranger."

I thought I should tell her, before she finished her story, that I'd been fired. That she had caught me as I was about to return to Sacramento and then head across the country in my car. She still looked through glass at the ocean.

Kate patted the back of her snug jeans. She found a smashed pack of Camels, fished out a cigarette and lit it. Kate tilted back her head and blew the first puff to the low cabin ceiling. She said, "I couldn't just stand by and let him squander money. He'd siphoned off almost sixty grand since we formed the new company." She blew a gray cloud upwards. "There, it's out. What I'm really worried about is some sicko could have killed my brother over money he owed, but couldn't get to." Kate shook her head, ran her hand, the cigarette burning between two fingers, across her forehead. "What

I mean is, somebody should look into this."

"I'm glad to hear you say that. I found footprints on the fire-break road above where your brother was hit. They look to me like—I must emphasize, they only look like two people were facing each other. They were fresh marks. I let myself free-fall from there down the hill. I ended up right where Senator Watkins hit your brother. It keeps bothering me."

Kate glanced sideways, blew cigarette smoke. She looked to be even less sure of herself than I was.

I stood and took a step toward her, remembering how when I was little and I'd wonder about who my dad was, I'd feel like a plaster of Paris dummy, hard on the outside, all chicken wire and air underneath, one crack and I could begin to crumble. I wanted to warn Kate about possible cracking. I wanted to tell her that if she would just keep going, day after day, her skin would grow thick, impenetrable, and she'd become accustomed to having a hollow place inside her, like I did.

"Look," I said, "I have to level with you. There's been a... Let's say there's been a difference of opinion as to how to proceed."

Kate Garston's teeth shone in white lines and this time when she chugged out cigarette smoke she laughed hoarsely. She said, "You city people are so full of shit." Her head swung in arcs, brown hair covering her face, her laugh turning giddy. "Why don't you just say you got fired?"

"How'd you know that?" I dropped back on the couch.

Kate said, "It's a small town."

I said, "Yeah, I guess. But my understanding is your family doesn't run it anymore."

Kate grinned madly and blew smoke through her nostrils. She said, "Oh, fuck you."

She spoke in a tone laced with camaraderie. I smiled and said, "Then fuck you, too."

She worked her hand into the right front pocket of her jeans and pulled out an envelope. Rolled into a cyclinder, a thick rubber band was doubled around it. She flipped the envelope at me.

I caught it with my half hand. The flap bulged open. "Is this for making you cry every time I see you?"

"It's what I could come up with without driving to Ukiah. Sixteen hundred and forty dollars. I can get more later."

Handling the envelope, I inhaled the lingering odor of cigarette smoke and a mustiness. It was as if the bills had come from moldy quarters, perhaps a long-locked drawer. I looked her in the eyes, waited for her to explain herself.

Kate Garston twirled brown hair to behind her left ear. She said, "I'm hiring you." She spied an empty coffee cup on the table, went to it and snuffed out the Camel.

With the roll of currency in my hook hand, I folded my arms across my chest, and shrugged. I was being offered good money to work the same job I had just been fired from. It was a hell of an ego boost. My worry was that Kate Garston was not rational and therefore not to be taken completely seriously.

Kate's hoarse voice said, "I want you to find out what happened to Joe. For now, as long as my mom's in town, I can't get involved. She's having enough trouble as it is. The best thing for her is to know Joe was drunk, Watkins was drinking, and what happened happened."

I set the money on the couch. I said, "Allan Watkins is an old buddy of the guy I've been working for. That guy helped me a lot. If I work for you, it would be seen as a betrayal."

Kate said, "For the sake of discussion, let's just say you work all that out in your head. Do what you can on your own the next four or five days, while Mom's in town. Anybody gives you guff, you can say you're working for me, but I don't want my mom to know about it. We've got to figure out if somebody killed Joe."

"You're not worried I'm going to take the money and just go?"

"If you do, I haven't lost anything important."

Kate went to the chair for her windbreaker. I didn't want her to leave.

I wanted to tell her that whatever had passed between us mattered to me. I put a hand on her shoulder. It felt good to touch her.

"Let me drive you. It's windy as hell out there."

She stepped away and slipped on the Gortex windbreaker. Kate said, "You feel sorry for me. That's not what I came for."

A shoulder brushed me as she passed. She went out the door. The gale slammed it shut. Suddenly I felt alone in a deep, sinking way that narrowed my vision. I stared out the window at ocean whitecaps lifted by wind.

Kate came into view. Her steps were brisk and her head bobbed up and down. The blue hood pointed skyward in a shiny cone. She walked a path lined with roundish boulders. She neared the bluff. Beyond her was the sea. I expected her to stop, to turn and locate my cabin.

Then I knew that was what I wanted Kate to do.

The blue hood dropped out of sight. My forehead pressed against the window. It was cool, comforting yet unyielding. I watched the spot where last I saw her.

Driving across the country in my car would mean more loneliness, long days and weeks alone. The loneliness I felt in Sunset County was oppressive, but at least it was familiar. For one of the few times in my life I was going to follow the desire of my heart and do what was right. I was going to find out if someone murdered Joe Garston. If someone had, I was going to nail the bastard.

I closed my eyes and imagined Kate Garston picking her way along the shoreline toward the skeletal remains of an old wood wharf. I saw her truck parked on the bluff above. I was already imagining myself into Kate's life. I saw us walking along a road amidst forest, on the hunt for her brother's killer. We were holding hands. In my head she didn't have on the windbreaker.

In my head she wore the tight jeans.

Seven

When I started kindergarten and saw that most of the other kids had two parents, my mom told me she and my father had gone out together for almost a year, and although she loved him she had never wanted to marry him. If Mom had lived in San Francisco or L.A. she might have been able to stay near family and friends after she became pregnant, but the 1996 values of Atwater, in the southern Sacramento Valley, were not much different from the town's collective values of 1976 or even 1956. To be an unwed mother in Atwater in 1996 meant everyone forgot your phone number.

So Mom left Atwater, five months pregnant, twenty years old, and moved to the northwestern corner of California. She joined a friend from high school who had moved there to be with a guy she'd met at a reggae concert. Their relationship hadn't lasted but she'd stayed on in Grantsville, population two thousand, living in a converted barn. Grantsville was an eclectic mix of loggers, old timers, ex-hippies and people like my mother who went somewhere to try to make new lives for themselves. My earliest memories are of Mom and me under blankets on the couch, listening to short wave radio in the barn. I remember that but more deeply I remember walking amidst towering virgin redwoods, some of the largest trees on earth. I remember the silence except for light sounds of our footsteps, the air so fresh it was like you were being pumped full of oxygen. It was the two of us in our own private world. We lived on what in Grantsville was still called welfare, which confirmed our status as outsiders.

Mom eventually got a part time waitressing job at The Blue Heron Café. I'd walk in the door at home after school and we'd leave for work. I ate dinner there and cleared tables. I grew tall early and taught myself how to shoot a basketball through a hoop better than any kid around, which gave me a standing in the community I otherwise would never have achieved. And my mom pretty much let me do whatever I wanted. She never questioned me about beer on my breath on Friday nights after games. My glory was leading the Grantsville Wildcats to a small-school state basketball championship my senior year.

Nothing like that had ever happened in Grantsville. College coaches checked into the North Country Motor Inn, the only motel in town. I was recruited by small colleges with solid teams, not big-time Division One schools. These coaches treated my mom like a prom queen, which she rightly found condescending and insulting because it came with the implicit message that we were a poor family with no father even on the periphery of the boy star. And that they were offering to do us a favor. For me there were no objections to the attention. My picture was in not just the nearest newspaper but the Redding, Eureka and Sacramento papers as well—all big cities to me. A couple of times little kids even stopped me on the street and asked for my autograph. Therefore I was nearly bursting with self-importance when, the day after graduation, Mom told me she was moving to Alaska with Del Beverage. Del was a seasonal salmon fisherman and handyman who had been going out with her off and on for a few years. He had the opportunity to be a line supervisor at a cannery in the fishing hub of Naknek, and asked my mother to go with him. Mom described her confidence in me, explained that she was thirty-seven and that if she didn't take a chance then she might never take one. A week later, Mom was gone.

Families offered to take me in, but I insisted on living alone in a tiny unoccupied cabin that was behind The Blue Heron Café until leaving for college in Sacramento. I spent many a day staring at the knotty pine ceiling, imagining a life rather than living one. Like most of us at seventeen, I was certain my future involved grand deeds. It seemed to me then, as it seemed to me during the hours I sat alone in the cabin at Greenwood after Kate Garston left on Sunday afternoon, that I would do something important in life, but it would be done alone, and that it was my fate to be an outsider.

Maybe, after all these years, bringing to justice someone who killed Joe Garston was the important thing I was meant to do. It was without question more important than any shots I'd made on basketball courts.

I texted Clint Sherman, telling him Kate Garston had hired me to investigate her brother's death. Since working for her conflicted with Sherman Investigations' work for the senator, I wrote that I needed to complete my break from the agency that had really begun on the first of the month. I promised to stop in and argue with him about it upon returning to Sacramento. I added that I could not ethically respond to any messages, as Clint worked for Senator Watkins, who was the only known link to Joe Garston's death.

I began my work for Kate by searching for her brother's ex. I called the ten listings for Wells in the phone book left on the cabin's little eating table. A cousin of Molly's told me she was living in a trailer on the outskirts of Ukiah. She didn't know the name of the trailer park. Molly, the cousin said, fronted a country and western band called The Wellbeats. They'd played the lounge shows in Reno, and once even in Las Vegas. When they traveled, the trailer was Molly's home on wheels.

I put a thousand dollars under the spare tire in the trunk of my Jetta and headed east, leaving redwoods after I climbed and then dropped over the ridge and drove through rolling hills covered with oaks and pine trees and Douglas fir. It was hot out. In an hour and a half I reached Ukiah. There was only one trailer park, a metal village sitting on lifeless soil between Highway 101 and the county dump. Molly Wells' silver travel trailer shone under sunlight, with *The Wellbeats* painted in red cursive on the side. Parked next to the trailer was a burgundy Chevy Bronco. On the rear of the Bronco was a heavy-duty trailer hitch.

Despite the hour, a dozen knocks and calls of her name were required to rouse Molly from sleep. Finally, the door to the trailer cracked open. Tiny fingers unhooked a latch. She swung the door inward. Light shot into the trailer.

She said, "Aw, shit," and retreated a few steps. Her hands flitted about her head like parakeets, shaping and patting long straight hair dyed a brassy red.

"Hello, Molly? Sorry if I woke you."

"Shit," she repeated, covering her face, knees drooping. She plopped backwards onto a grayish couch. "You said *after* the show." Her voice was high and flickering, and coarse at the same time. Molly said, "You bring a camera in here, I'll sue your ass."

On the nearby highway, Labor Day weekend vacationers rolled south, heading home. I spoke over the carry of engines. "I think you have me confused with somebody else. I don't know what you're talking about." Ducking under the steel doorframe, I stepped past Molly and was inside.

She looked up. "You got a camera guy out there? If you do, give me ten minutes. I can work up a good shot in ten."

The inside of the trailer was smaller than the outside made you think it would be. It felt like being in a crowded mini submarine. The air smelled of sour liquor and cigarettes. The sink overflowed with dirty dishes. I sat across from her, folded my hands, and acted like being there was as normal as the sunny day.

Mascara was smeared around her shiny black eyes. She tugged a short blue robe over white legs. Her face was round, the black eyes set above a short, upturned nose. Molly had what I guess you'd call average looks, but the smeared makeup and flashy red hair gave her a suggestive aura.

Molly said, "Who the hell are you? What time is it?"

"It's twenty-six minutes after five."

She swung the bright hair. Molly said, "I didn't get to bed till one. This afternoon." She grabbed a pink pillow from the corner of the couch and slid it over her legs. Her voice leaped: "You got I.D.? I promised Sacramento channel three an exclusive. KRON in SF comes next. After that I might talk to you, but I don't know if you're from a paper, TV or one of these internet places."

I showed her my driver's license. "This is all I have. The short version of why I'm here is, I'm looking into the death of Joe Garston."

Molly pressed the back of a twiggy wrist to her forehead like it was a compress. She spoke theatrically. "Oh, now don't tell me. Let me guess." The brassy hair draped down the front of her. "Yes, I think I got it." She shot me a look of bored contempt. "You're one of two ilks. You can be working for an ambulance-chasing lawyer, who's planning to screw me, or my sister-in-law, who I bet's planning the same."

Molly sat back. She folded her arms in a posed way I took to be making fun of me. "Well, handsome?"

"You win. Kate Garston hired me to find out what happened to your ex-husband."

"Husband, Sherlock. And you tell the Tree Queen to remember that."

"I just had the impression you and Joe were divorced, because you didn't live together."

Molly crossed her white legs under the pillow. She nibbled at her lower lip, then hopped to her feet and shut the trailer door. She raised some blinds, letting in light. She said, "I'm going for a cancer stick," and stepped down a short narrow hallway.

She opened the bathroom door behind her, as a partition between where I sat and the bedroom of the trailer. I heard drawers open and shut, and tossed garments hit the floor. I scanned the room. Most of the wall space was covered with posters announcing past appearances by The Wellbeats. In them Molly's hair was topped by a white cowboy hat and she wore a white leather jacket that had long tassels running up the arms, a white tasseled miniskirt and shiny knee-high white boots. She smiled as though somebody had prompted her to. Behind her, three cowpokes mugged for the camera.

I surveyed the clutter, dishes, movie magazines, filled ashtrays, a wadded black bra in a corner on the floor. Across from the built-in chair I sat on was a counter with a television set on it. Atop the TV was unopened mail.

Molly went into the bathroom. I heard her peeing into a metal toilet. I took a step out of the chair and perused her mail. Nothing but junk. On the brown plastic counter next to the TV were two empty sixteen-ounce Budweiser beer cans. One had a dark lipstick smudge, the other did not. I remembered the beer can I'd found on the road near where Joe Garston had been hit: a sixteen-ounce Bud.

The door flew open and Molly came out wearing black spike heels that clicked across linoleum. She waved a lighted cigarette and talked rapidly. "You people are all alike. You know that? You want stuff."

She sat opposite me again. Above the black heels she wore thin black leggings you could partly see through. Next up was a long black-and-white polka-dot top pulled close to her frame by a black belt. She glowed with nervous energy.

I said, "What people are all alike?"

Molly brought the filtered cigarette to her lips. She kissed it more than she inhaled, and her hand waved at trailing smoke. Her lips were covered with plum-colored lipstick. She said, "You seem like a nice guy." She reached over and tapped the bicep of my right arm. "Hey," she said, "I'm supposed to call my lawyer when stuff like this comes up. But all it does is cost me money. He logs talk. See, lawyers log talk like the Tree Queen logs trees. Between the two of them, I'm afraid I'm going to get thrown under the bus."

She sprang from the gray couch and clicked through the hallway. She pulled open the metal bathroom door behind her again.

"Hey, Molly. Is it all right if I call you Molly?"

"Do it on a trial basis, we'll see how it goes." I heard something get knocked over in the bedroom compartment.

I said, "Why don't you let me take you out for an early dinner? Before you do anymore coke. Maybe we could slow things down a little."

On the other side of the door, the bustling ceased.

I said, "What do you say? I can ask questions and you can ignore them. At least you'll get a decent meal out of it."

Molly pushed the door closed ahead of her. In the four-inch heels, she didn't seem so small. She nodded, slowly, and nibbled at her lower lip. The coke smile had evaporated. I stood. Outside, traffic droned. I swallowed over a raw dryness and tasted Molly's sultry perfume. Her eyes glowed like embers. For one long, exhilarating second, I thought Molly was either going to propose we have sex or pull a knife from behind her and stab me.

Her round face fell into a sad, contemplative gaze. Molly said, "That's the worst part." Her voice was not much louder than a whisper. "I'm going through all this crap and I don't have anybody to really talk to about it. I got a good lawyer—he's a shark, but nobody to sort it all out with. The guy I'm seeing, he doesn't want to hear about it. The last thing he wants to talk about is a husband I didn't divorce."

Molly sniffed, twitched her upturned nose.

I said, "That's horrible." I put my hands on her bony shoulders, guided her down to her seat, let go and sat back myself. I acted in a way designed to convince Molly that I wanted to help her sort things out. "Listen, do you have any food in here? Maybe we could rustle up something. I don't feel like talking in public anymore. It's not really my thing, anyway."

After I let go of her shoulders, Molly saw my bad hand. Her right hand went to her lips. "Oh, God. I'm... I didn't mean to stare. I'm..."

I helped. "It's okay. Let's go back to me realizing I don't want to go out somewhere. See what we can rustle up."

Molly said, "Sounds good."

She touched the cigarette to her lips, twisted her lips sideways and blew smoke toward the short narrow hallway. I wondered if this was the first time since Joe died that she had stopped the nonsense chatter, the cocaine and booze and whatever other poisons kept her motor running.

I went to the eating area, opened the mini refrigerator. You couldn't feed a squirrel on what was inside.

Her voice cracked as she said, "I just want some OJ."

I said, "Coming right up."

I turned to her, smiled. Part of me detested Molly for talking about money when only the day before her ex-husband, or husband, had been killed. Part of me detested myself for playing along with her. She smiled back, blew more smoke sideways. I shook the dregs of orange juice.

I said, "I know we can come up with a meal in this place. Go ahead, what do you want?"

Molly grinned a sad, stony grin. She swung her long hair languidly, like a fan. "A little vodka in that OJ wouldn't hurt my feelings. You'll find some in the cabinet above the microwave."

Three inches remained in a generic bottle. I poured the vodka into the orange juice carton and gave it a shake. I wondered if she knew more than she wanted to reveal. It would account for the nervous trips to the back for cocaine.

I took a swig, handed the carton to Molly. "Saluda. And beware, it's fifty-fifty vodka."

Molly downed two swallows with her eyes open. She handed me the plum-lipstick-smudged container.

I said, "If this is your idea of dinner, I can see how you keep your figure."

Molly looked at me with bat's eyes that had regained their

luminosity. "You know what that son of a bitch said? The one the senator who killed Joe sent to the gig last night?"

I brought the carton to my mouth. I made a show of taking a swallow but drank nothing. "I wouldn't put anything past those people. They're not to be trusted."

Molly reached for the carton. In the exchange, our brows tapped. She sat back and drank. "This guy said a lot of crap. Stuff about how he wanted me to tell some newspaper chick I thought Joe was killed by somebody. Like it was a murder, a real murder, not an accident." Her voice rose and fell, and a countrified slur crept into it. "God that man talked fast. I don't know what-all he was saying. He wanted to drive me over to the coast—just like that, in his car. He said I'd be on TV. Like three stations were waiting to interview me. Can you believe it?"

I nodded truthfully though without sympathy. Molly knocked back the drink. She peered into the carton and exhaled vodka fumes. She finished her cigarette and ground it out in a glass ashtray. Tears messed the fresh mascara. I speculated about the battle going on inside her, feelings of loss versus the desire for financial gain. How badly, over time, would it taint her?

Molly didn't bother drying her tears. She said, "You got religion? I seen Mormons clean cut like you. And you got, you know, the hand thing."

"I was paid to find out if anybody other than Allan Watkins killed your husband."

Molly took a section of her flowing hair and draped it down her left arm. With her right hand she smoothed the hair, like you would a towel before folding it. She watched the motion of her hand. This seemed to help her think. "A guy like you," she said. "A guy like you would never have trouble making money. Not if it's what you really wanted. You're not doing this for the money."

She smiled, gathered the hair in her right hand and tossed it over her shoulder, leaned forward and tapped me on the knee. Her eyes were oiled by the vodka on top of cocaine. It seemed they wanted to tell me something Molly herself couldn't get out. Her eyes searched me all over. Her mouth moved some, and she winced like she'd stepped on a tack. I could tell she wasn't going to cry, but I thought she might open up to me.

Her tongue darted between the smeared-plum lips.

I shook my head, to throw off some of the tension locking us together. I said, "Let's get some food in that stomach of yours. I think I just heard it growl."

Molly giggled, sounding like a whinnying colt, swung the metallic hair—and a booming weight hit the stairs attached below the trailer's door. She turned to me, showing fear, as though I would know who it was. Knocking rattled the door.

"Molly-dew? You in there, yes? I don't want to, but I got to ask you a few questions."

Molly raced to the door and swung it open. "Cliffy!"

She almost disappeared inside the folds of Sheriff Niles' belly and chest. He stepped in, holding her airborne, and set her on the spike heels. Sheriff Niles was sweating at the temples of his graying hair. "Honey," he said, doughy eyelids falling and rising, "I'm sorry. You know I'm sorry we have to have this kind of talk."

I stood. Niles twitched at registering my presence.

Molly said, "I'm so glad you're here!"

I gave the sheriff a breezy wave of my good hand.

Niles shot me a pained grin. His face appeared buttery in the half-light of the trailer.

"Aw, shit," Molly said. "This don't look right."

Niles' right arm was being hugged as if he were a stuffed animal. He leaned to his left. Sheriff Niles said, "I was led to believe you went back to Sacramento."

"It's a long story."

"Sure, brother. Whatever you say."

Molly said, "He says he's working for the Tree Queen."

"I am."

Niles burst into jiggling laughter. He disentangled himself from Molly, made a quick examination of the submarine-like trailer. He wore a tan cop's uniform. He dropped onto the brown couch across from me. He looked at me like he was trying to make a decision. He looked at me like he could kick my ass if he wanted to.

Molly shot me an inquisitive gape, then gave Cliff Niles the same quizzical gaze.

Niles grinned. "You got to tell me. How did you and Kate get hooked up?"

"I guess she made me feel needed."

He shook his jowls, ignored my answer. "Molly-Dew? You got any water?" Niles lifted his big square nose and sniffed. "It smells like a bar in here. After hours."

I pondered the physical intensity of their greeting.

At the sink, Molly ran tap water into a coffee cup and handed it to the sheriff. She said, "We haven't been partying. Promise. We had one to start the day. I mean evening. And then this brute is going to do a magic trick and make us dinner from my little freezer." Standing because there was no place for her to sit, Molly grimaced playfully. It was subtle, and I would guess without forethought: Molly shook her booty.

Niles said, "Jeff's going to make you dinner? Why that's right thoughtful of him. Extremely," Niles said, in a tone indicating doubt, "thoughtful of him."

"Actually," I said, "I'd like to whip up a miracle for you, Molly. But the truth is the sheriff would cramp my style. I couldn't ask you the insulting questions I would if it were just the two of us. Besides," I said, standing, "I've got a couple of places to go tonight."

Molly said, "C'mon. We got like a stay-cation date."

"I'd really like to take a rain check. You two should be able to talk alone."

Molly hit Niles on the shoulder. "Why don't you tell him he's on a goose chase? You and I both know Joe must've walked home blitzed a hundred times."

Niles wrapped a meaty hand around her wrist. "I can't do that, Honey." He rose, stepped toward me, and while he was a lot shorter than I am his girth forced me toward the door. Niles said, "I got to have a report on the DA's desk in the morning."

Molly's mouth opened. Her head spun back and forth between Niles and me.

I said to her, "I'm sure we'll get together soon." I jokingly blew Molly a kiss, and stepped outside into yellow sunlight. The metal door banged shut behind me.

Eight

I sat in the car, thinking. Niles goes to church with his wife. Eight hours later he shows up in Ukiah wearing a cop's uniform. Was there anything suspicious about that? No. He was there on official business. He had driven over in a patrol car. But there was no denying the oddness of Molly Wells jumping into his arms, no denying it was peculiar Niles called her "Molly Dew." And "Honey" didn't exactly sound like standard police protocol.

I started my dark Jetta and chased the sun. By the time I reached the coast the sky was a deepening purple. I parked near where Joe Garston was hit, and looked for the empty can of Budweiser I'd picked up the day before. I wanted to see if it had lipstick marks. The can was gone. I checked both sides of the road. The wakes of cars and trucks could have blown it anywhere. I looked in weeds part way up the hillside.

I went to Garston's bloodstains, already fading, scarcely visible in the waning dusk. The marks we leave on this earth disappear fast. From there I ascended the hill, pushed through the wall of crackling brush and located the circle of boot prints. I had no plan as to how to go about an investigation, and thought returning to the scene of the theoretical crime was a good place to start. I sat under the spreading dark wings of a large cypress tree.

I took out the compact notebook I always carry in a back pocket, and scribbled the names of everyone I had spoken with since arriving in Sunset. By free association I listed words describing some of them. Next I drew lines connecting who I knew had spoken to whom, Welty-Niles, Kate Garston-Bobby Stiving, Niles-Molly, Molly and presumably Welty. It seemed important to track lanes of communication, to see if a pattern emerged.

I flipped the page and began a list of tasks so crudely half-hand scrawled that probably only I could read them. *Go to Art's. Talk to Kolatch. Talk to Stiving with Kate there. Clerk Simpson, first impressions when Senator was brought in? Anything he said sticks out?* I put down the notebook because, in the minute between cars passing below, I remembered what quiet is. I remembered it from when I was a kid. It was like a drug: all muscles relaxed. I stretched back under the tree and closed my eyes. I'd been moving nonstop for two days.

My mind drifted. I saw pieces of the roads I'd driven over to Ukiah and back, vistas, turns, groves of redwoods in shadowy creek canyons, cloudless pale sky. I heard the tinny foreign voices you sometimes hear when falling asleep—and sat up fast. It was now dark. Something was coming toward me. Footsteps? Maybe a lot of footsteps.

I hopped up. I stepped out from under the tree and called, "Hello? Hello? Who's there?"

The noises stopped.

My adrenaline kicked into racing gear. I crossed crackling dead grass to the dirt road. I saw shapes in the near blackness of tree cover, but couldn't make out anything specific.

"Who are you? Come on, no games."

Nothing. I was about a hundred feet from where I perceived the shapes, and as I stepped toward them, they moved away, though not far. I kept moving forward. My pincer hand opened and closed reflexively.

I yelled, "Goddamn it, cut the crap. Who are you?"

I walked toward the dark shapes. They were a family. Three deer. Their rubbery necks turned, following me, their six eyes glowing circles surrounded by night. They turned and trotted north along the fire break road.

I jogged after them, laughing. The deer scattered.

God, I thought, am I getting paranoid or what?

I walked for awhile, wide awake now, thinking about Senator Watkins. During my college days he was the most talked about legislator in seminars on state government. He was a hero to a lot of us. Watkins was seen as a man who would ignore changes in the political climate and work his own combination of liberal/centrist legislation while avoiding the endless battles over abortion, race and sexuality. He was a kind of meat and potatoes liberal, and he got things done.

He was also a man about whom stories were told.

One often repeated was the time Watkins fell out an open window while chatting with the United States Secretary of Agriculture in the banquet room of the Capitol Hilton. Watkins had been leaning back against the windowsill, yakking, and leaned back too far. It was said he landed in juniper bushes, didn't spill a drop of his martini nor for one second cease his pitch for more low-interest loans from Washington to California alfalfa farmers to ease them through a drought. And there was the time, under the headline "The Pang of Four," a columnist reported on a night Watkins had commandeered a speedboat with the intention of racing himself and three buddies up the Sacramento River to a favored backwater bar in rural Yolo County. He pulled up at the wrong dock and barking German shepherds leaped aboard. Two elected officials ended up in the river. Watkins, according to the article, put his hands out, and when the dogs didn't bite, he calmed them by rubbing behind their ears.

While in school I thought these were great stories. I still thought they were great stories. However, after working for Clint Sherman and seeing Watkins at various functions around the capitol city, my attitude toward him changed. In the same way pro athletes are less interesting once they begin to talk about their game rather than play it, Watkins was more interesting in lore than in the flesh.

Dark as it had become, it wasn't hard to follow the dirt road and find my way back. I located the cypress tree I'd been under. Using a pen light, searching through needles and dead grass and bark bits, I couldn't find my notebook. I finally dropped down the hill to my car. I came back with my big round yellow flashlight. Wherever I pointed it I could see clearly. Yes, I was looking under the right tree. The truth of things seeped through me. Someone, though possibly some animal, had taken the notebook.

This time the adrenaline rush sang with fear. Who had been out there, close enough to know I'd been writing in a notebook under that tree? The person who murdered Joe Garston, that was who. There were other possibilities, of course, but until I was in my car heading down the coast highway, I was too scared to think of them. All I could think about was that if those deer hadn't clomped along, and I had fallen completely asleep under the cypress, I might have met the same fate as Joe.

Nine

Art's was in a former Moose Hall a block off the coast highway. The place was mobbed. Rather than mirrors, like a regular bar, Art's had hubcaps on the wall beyond the long wooden service counter. They threw off warped images. I plowed my way through revelers, bounced left off one and found a slot near the end of the counter.

After talking with Hal, bartender at The Cove, I had expected Art's to be a kind of low-rent pizza joint. But Art's turned out to be the social hub in Sunset County if you were under forty. At pine tables sat the younger members of ranching clans, plumbers, realtors, nail pounders, and people employed in the marijuana industry. Several were attractive women in tank tops who looked like they could wrestle. There were men sporting earrings and women sporting nose rings. There were a lot more tattoos than you'd see at the opera.

A jukebox blasted souped-up country music. I got a beer and took gulps. My head still swam: somebody had been hiding above where Joe Garston had died. Somebody had gone under the cypress tree and stolen my notebook.

Who? Why?

I swallowed tap beer and looked around. The smell of steaming pizzas and garlic bread made my stomach cry for a feeding, but I was too cranked up to eat. I figured out who was boss of the two guys behind the long wooden bar, and tipped my head, calling him over. I asked for another beer and this time dropped a fifty.

As though I were wearing a sign, he said, "You must be here about Joe."

He had a big, freckled face. Dark red hair fell at an angle across his forehead. He was half-swacked.

"That's right," I said, leaning forward, trying to be confidential. "I'd like to ask you a few questions."

He refilled my glass and brought me change for the fifty.

I said, "Art, right? I'm not expecting change from you."

He said, "I'm not expecting shit from you. Or maybe I am. But I won't take money with it." He didn't seem concerned that someone would hear him.

He left the two twenties and four ones on the bar. People to both sides of me were engaged in loud conversations. Quickly checking them out I got dizzy. I said, "I'm not a cop." I adjusted my feet, found my balance. "I'm not from an insurance company. I don't work for any lawyers."

He said, "If you're expecting a gold medal, you came to the wrong place."

"I just want to level with you."

Art made a slow, drunken martial arts cut through the hazy air between us. "Level away. On the level."

"I'm working for Joe Garston's sister. If you'll tell me everything that happened here Friday night, I'll keep paying for beers with fifties."

Art waved off some hooting from the far end of the bar. He leaned against his side the counter. "Give me some I.D."

I handed Art my wallet, using my left hand so as not to distract him. It bulged with greenbacks. He opened it, closed an eye to scrutinize my driver's license.

"You're from Sacramento." He flipped through everything. "You got a bunch of cards from a detective shop."

I made a mental note to dispose of the Sherman Investigations business cards.

He looked up with red-streaked eyes. "You got a load of dough, but it doesn't look like it came with you. City money's cleaner than this."

The acuteness of this observation surprised me. I thought I better listen, though it was hard to hear him over the din. I said, "That money's part of what Kate Garston gave me to retrace her brother's last steps. Seriously, you can have some. That's what it's for."

He snapped the wallet shut and flipped it at me. It hit me on the chest. He ran a hand over his clammy red face, then drained beer into his mouth. The people next to me were shouting with exuberance about something I couldn't catch. I felt surrounded.

Art said, "You should've been here earlier. B-B Stiving was in. He knew Joe better than anybody. He was up on the ranch when it happened, or maybe you already know that. They had B-B go in and tell Kate."

I said, "I've talked with B-B." I tapped at the bruises on my left cheek and lips.

Art said, "Ah, so you have. I didn't see. It's these goddamn dim lights. Well, at least you still got your teeth."

"How long ago did Stiving leave?"

"About an hour. Maybe more. I was just coming on shift. He wasn't drinking. He's been pretty quiet these past two days. He's taking it hard."

I finished my beer. I was feeling better. After all, I hadn't been stabbed or shot or anything, and as was pointed out, I still had my teeth. Art brought me a fresh beer in a frosted mug, and I didn't try to push the money bit. I lifted the mug. I used my right hand. It seemed too dark for anyone to notice its peculiarities.

I said, "May Joe Garston rest in peace."

It felt good to be in Art's. Maybe that's what I needed, or at least yearned for: a world where others didn't notice exterior defects obscuring what is beneath. Hell, I guess what I needed was to believe the heart mattered more than my ability to make a symmetrical right fist.

Art went to serve other customers. When he returned, he pointed a damp finger at me and said, "I'm talking to you out of respect for the family. They've done a lot of good for this county, whether people like Kate Garston or not."

Art told me Joe had come in around nine on Friday, his usual time four or five nights a week. He had come in alone, which was also as usual. He went from table to table, not really part of any group but not really rejected by anyone.

Art said, "Joe may have been an asshole, but we're in it together around here. Even if he got on your nerves now and then, he wasn't a bad guy. Joe just drank too much, like a lot of us, and he had too much free time on his hands. In a way he was a rich kid, and in a way he wasn't. The Garstons still own all that property, but they probably don't net much more in a year than I do. And mind you, I ain't no Warren Buffett or Mark Zuckerbobo."

He brought us fresh beers, had a sip from the frosted glass.

"Okay," I said, "I think I have an idea what kind of guy Joe was. But if you could, Friday night, go back and tell me what he did. Anything you can remember."

Dice rattled on the bar. Behind me people danced and stomped and clapped hands.

"Well, he did one thing I thought of after I heard he got hit. It might be nothing, but it sticks out."

I was jostled from the side but ignored it. Art said that about midnight Joe gave him three one-dollar bills and asked for quarters. Then he'd walked out the front door.

Art said, "The last phone booth in town is about a five-minute walk from here, at the corner of the highway and Sunset Avenue. I didn't ask him, and he didn't say, but he must have gone out to make a phone call. I'm thinking, his last name's Garston and he don't have a cell phone? Then it hits me Joe probably didn't pay his bill."

"Did he come back in?"

"No. It was the last anybody around here saw him."

"Do you have any idea who he would have called? Assuming he made a call."

"That's just it, man. I figured he got lonesome and was calling Molly. You know who I'm talking about?"

I told Art that Molly and I were acquainted.

"He used to call her once in a while when he got fongoed. He'd come back in and complain about whatever the hell they'd just fought about. Molly was most likely playing music somewhere, it being Friday night. Do you know she's got a band?" I recited the band's name. Art said, "Not bad, buddy. Anyway, I figure she's out playing music somewhere, and he calls her and leaves a message. That's my guess."

"Besides Molly, who else would he call?"

Art said, "Most everybody he knew was here. The only other person would be B-B, for a ride. But that don't wash because Joe ended up walking home. I don't know what happened. But giving him three bucks in quarters, it sticks out."

Above and behind Art's head were the hubcaps. Looking into them I saw distorted, smoky reflections of the crowd. My face felt hot. I said the first thing that came to mind.

"Who would want to kill him?"

Art turned his body a bit to the side. His eyes narrowed into red slits as they locked onto mine. He wiped his face. "What was that?"

"Is there anybody who would like to see Joe Garston dead?"

This time his arm cut a slow, big X in the air. For some reason it reminded me of skywriting. Art said, "You're out of bounds, man. Way out of bounds. You want to talk like that, go see the sheriff."

He headed down the bar, back to work.

"Art! I think you got this wrong."

My voice was thick, too loud. People looked at me, waited for a response from Art. He didn't give one. At the far end of the bar he brought two tall glasses of beer to friendly customers. Foam spilled over the edges like waves. He looked small, far away. I was fairly smashed;

fatigue and fright had sent the beer straight to my brain. Someone tapped me on the shoulder and I jumped about a foot in the air.

"Hey, Jeff, take it easy."

It was a woman's voice, warm, soothing—for a second I thought it was Kate Garston. Blood punched through my head as though screaming to get out. I turned.

She said, "Remember me?"

A black felt hat presided over light skin, a freckled face. Her gray eyes were shaped like almonds. A black leotard top was tucked into jeans. I wondered where I knew her from, and blinked and shook my head, trying to retrieve a name.

She said, "Don't you remember me?"

I said, "What are *you* doing up here on the coast?"

"I'm enjoying the universe." Her voice was airy, happy. She added, "Besides, I live here."

"How long have you lived out here?" I took a swallow of beer and looked around, hoping like hell there wouldn't be a whole group with her that would respond to my presence in the vein of Bobby Stiving. Bobby the Bear.

She said, "I'm Anne Simpson, you drunken dope. You gave me a bunch of money yesterday to bail out Allan Watkins."

"Of course." I suddenly felt cooler. She was no ghost from the past. "I guess I'm a little buzzed. Sorry. I, uh…" I leaned over and tweaked the rim of her black hat. To her ear, I said, "Are you here under cover?"

"What does it look like?"

"It looks wonderful."

Anne said, "Can't you do any better than that?" Her laugh took off like a run up piano keys. Anne Simpson grabbed the black felt hat and secured it on her head.

I said, "I've been wanting to talk to you."

We were jostled by the reaction to a joke somewhere behind her. The place was even more packed than when I arrived. Anne Simpson took hold of my elbow and led me to beneath wooden stairs that climbed to what must have been an office. We sat facing each other at a pine table. A string of red and blue bulbs was tacked along the wall a few feet above her head.

She said, "No offense, but you look a little green around the gills."

"I'm doing the best I can."

A waitress sashayed by, tray in hand, dark hair held up in a whalebone clip. I flagged her down.

"Yes?"

"Could you get us a large pizza with everything?"

She clicked a pen and wrote on a pad that was on the tray. The waitress said, "One large combo. Anything else?"

Anne said, "Two bottles of Anchor Steam."

The waitress left, negotiating the crowd like a kayak running rapids.

Anne said, "I'm having fun. Are you having fun?"

I said, "I am not having fun."

She reached over and touched my bruised mouth. "That's right. I hear you got in a fight with B-B." She examined my whole face.

"I don't care about that. I'm just tired. This has been the longest day of my life."

I saw her and wavering shadows. Beneath the black hat her eyes gave off a flinty light. Freckles dotted her nose. Russet hair fell straight, framing her light face.

I said, "Why are you staring at me? Most people stare at my hand. Maybe I should get the shit kicked out of me more often, so people will notice that instead of my hand. Wait, I'm serious, why are you staring?"

Anne said, "I'm not sure how to proceed."

"I have an idea." I stretched my legs under the table, and found her feet. "Why don't you follow me to the cabin I'm staying at? I'll turn the hot water on, and we can take a bubble bath. They left a fresh bottle." The beer glass in my hand was empty. I slid it across the pine table. "We could we make that pizza to go. It'd be a platonic bubble bath. You have my word."

Anne Simpson took off her hat and set it atop my empty glass. She said, "You know I'm going to say no, but you still ask. I don't get it."

"I don't think I get it, either. I'm not exactly of sound mind right now. Let's delete the fake flirt."

The waitress came with two brown bottles of beer. Anne must have seen her gliding our way because she had money out before I could reach for my wallet.

I said, "Let me back up a bit. Did you come here with anybody?"

"No."

"How long have you been here?"

"About an hour. That's five questions so far. Twenty minus five means you've got fifteen left."

I lifted the amber bottle, clinked hers and had a swallow. "Did you see Bobby Stiving tonight?"

"I hope you're not looking for a re-match. I don't think it's a good idea."

"As my mother used to say, 'I may be ignorant but I'm not stupid.'"

"Good to know," Anne said.

"Seriously, was Stiving here when you arrived?"

"No, but I saw him. Actually, I saw his truck. It was going north when I came into town."

"So he was heading toward the Garstons?"

"That direction, yes." Anne took a slug of beer. "He could've been going anywhere."

A song came on the jukebox. I asked her to dance. I added, "Let's go slow. Anything fast I'll fall over."

She put her hat on, and out we went. I held her close as I dared. I felt her skin through the black leotard. I bent over and nuzzled my face into the back of her shoulder and for a second, while swaying to the music—under the smell of Anne's skin and food—for a moment I thought I smelled trees. Could she have taken my notebook? When I pulled away to look at her and maybe say something silly about her hat, I also looked for a piece of leaf or cypress tree needles.

77

Anne tilted the brim of her hat against my chest. She said, "Dance with me. You're touching me like a creepy doctor."

I put my lips to her ear. "I'll do anything you want, if you'll answer another question."

Anne didn't say anything, but she stayed close as we made a turn with the music.

Aware people were watching me and a home-town woman on the dance floor, I whispered, "Do you think somebody pushed Garston down that hill?"

She whispered into my chest, "Why do you think I'm here?"

We danced another slow song, not talking. I held her like I'd known her for years. This included being careful with my right hand around her waist. If I squeezed it felt like, I'd been told, a claw of thumb and forefinger, more threatening than affectionate. I'd learned to be aware of that damnable hand at almost every moment. What it looked like always haunted the edge of my consciousness. A fast song came on and we made our way off the dance floor. Our beers were empty. I turned to look for help; the waitress was bringing steaming pizza and two white plates. She set everything down, along with the remaining change from a second fifty I had left at the bar. I asked for two more bottles of Anchor Steam.

I broke apart pizza slices, set one on Anne's plate. "Who do you think could've done it?"

She burned her finger on hot grease. She blew on it. This simple act was lovely, somehow classy. Anne said, "I know I didn't do it. I don't think you did it. Beyond that, the only strong feeling I have is I don't think Joe would have been standing in the middle of the road. If he was that blitzed, he wouldn't have gotten a mile out of town."

Anne took a swallow from her bottle.

I said, "Is it possible he committed suicide?"

"Joe? No guts."

We ate pizza and got down to business. I told her about being fired; Kate showing up at Greenwood and hiring me; driving to Ukiah and

78

talking to Molly Wells; going to the accident site at dusk; drifting off almost to sleep; the deer waking me; chasing them and then returning to find my notebook swiped. I told her it scared the hell out of me. I told Anne everything except my earlier thought that she might possibly be the notebook thief.

I expected all of this to make quite an impression, but none of it got much of a reaction. She ate, sipped beer, nodded. So I asked her to tell me what she knew. She wiped her mouth with a fresh napkin, nodded once more. "All I know is, Kate gets what she wants. She always has and she probably always will."

I said, "Don't try to tell me she wanted her brother dead. First of all, she wouldn't have hired me to look into things. And second, hell, I know he caused her a lot of trouble, but I just won't buy it."

Anne cleaned her fingers with the paper napkin. "Look-it, Jeff. I'm not saying anything specific. I'm just saying a good starting point for me is what does Kate want? Over the years, whatever the situation, it seems like she ends up with what she wanted in the first place."

I'd become numb to the crowd noise and blasting music. I raised my good hand to order another round. Anne said she had to be going.

I said, "You could do a good deed by leading me down to Greenwood. Would you? I'm not sure I'll able to find it. Not in my current condition."

"Drive with one eye closed." Anne stood, and fiddled with her black hat. "We learn that young around here."

I stood. We smiled back and forth. I saw Anne well enough to recognize interest on her face. I also didn't want to return to a strange room for a beer-spinning, lonely sleep.

I touched the tops of her shoulders, then gently massaged the back of her neck. "What if I promise I won't... get pushy. Not even close. Would it work?"

Anne said, "I can't answer that."

"Why not?"

She rose on tiptoes and kissed me on a cheek. Her lips were cool from beer, though I thought I felt something warmer than what had poured into her from frosted mugs.

I said, "Really, why won't you come with me?"

Anne said, "Sorry. You ran out of questions."

She disappeared into smoke.

Ten

At noon a housekeeper banged on the door. He told me it was time to go. The cabin had been rented by another party months before. I left a tip and drove to town. I grew coherent over a second coffee at Connie's Home Baked, wishing Sheriff Niles were there. I wanted to trade impressions of our separate talks with Molly Wells, see what information, or even hints, I could glean from him. After reading a fair if somewhat lurid account of the accident and Senator Watkins' history with booze in the *San Francisco Chronicle*, I walked down the block to Sunset Outfitters. I spent almost four hundred dollars buying gear. I was taking up residence at the county campground. On my phone I read that an overflow field was set up to accommodate more visitors than was normal, no running water, and distant porta-potties for restrooms. It seemed they could accommodate all comers in what was a strategy to combat people from pitching tents in private woods and leaving their garbage behind.

At a used bookstore I found a copy of *Democracy in America*, Alexis de Tocqueville's masterpiece. History 17A stuff, the kind of reading I like. I drove to my next home. Sunlight warmed my hands as I set up camp. Square spaces were chalked off like slots at a flea market. I was about as far away from amenities as one could get but it meant I was closer to stately redwood trees that were brushed by wind. Reddish needles rained to the ground like confetti. Autumn was approaching. Garston Creek was quiet that late in the year, a somber green. I hiked upstream to the swimming hole Niles had mentioned. Half a mile in from the ocean, the air was dry. Gray stones baked. Young bodies stretched flat on the bank like seals. Dogs barked and chased Frisbees into the water. I swam till my arms hurt, listening closely. I didn't hear the words, "Joe Garston."

Tuesday morning I heated water over a campfire for a shave, and washed up in the stream. I drove to the county government complex, the series of redwood buildings where I had posted bail for Senator Watkins.

I was prepared for a circus, but a small one with no exotic acts, because it was after a long holiday weekend and Sunset was five hours by car from San Francisco or Sacramento, and two hours from the nearest airport. I was wrong. There were about ten vans with satellite dishes on top. Thick cables snaked along pavement to cameras and microphones. Among the shirt-sleeved technicians and newspaper reporters were people wearing TV makeup, the talking heads. One woman wore a crimson blazer, blood-colored earrings that looked like fishing lures, and a clear plastic bag over her hair to save its coiffure from the wind. A guy about forty, in a dark banker's suit and pancake makeup, studied notes and fingered a maroon tie. There were at least fifty gawkers, probably mostly locals out to see what all the fuss was about. They faced the concrete steps of City Hall, which was on the opposite side of the parking lot from the Sheriff's Department, slightly uphill.

I parked toward the rear of the lot. I went up to a guy about thirty, wearing a brown Peterbilt baseball cap, who leaned back against his pickup of the same color. He spit oily tobacco juice into a Styrofoam coffee cup.

I said, "What's happening?"

He said, "Fuckers pulled one on us." He spat another oily stream and wiped his mouth. He clearly hadn't combed his greasy hair in days. "They changed the hearing to eight without telling anybody. He gets to sneak in before the peoples are here. Ain't that a dog?"

I said, "You know how politicians are."

He spit into the Styrofoam cup. "Can't say as I do. I only know they're shitheads who try to tell a man what he can or cannot do with his property. You can't put in a septic tank without paying big bucks to an engineer to plan it, an architect to draw it, and a permit from the county. They bleed you to death when all you want to do is flush your fuckin' toilet."

I scanned the crowd. If Joe's killer had returned to the scene of the crime to steal my notebook, he could just as easily turn up at the Senator's preliminary hearing. While looking for someone who stood out from the crowd as alone and anxious, it hit me that any of a dozen reporters could have been hiding in the woods near where I had sat under the cypress, keeping watch on the death site. Was one of them was the notebook thief?

Paul Raymer, an ex-marine and Sherman Investigations' premier muscle, stood at the bottom of the courthouse steps. He, too, checked the crowd for weirdos, his face both grim and friendly. I retreated. The last thing I wanted was for Raymer to stride through the throng and ask me why in the hell was I working for Kate Garston. I knew I owed Clint Sherman more loyalty than I was giving him. I hid between a couple of white vans with TV station acronyms painted on their sides, out of Raymer's sight line.

A seawater breeze came from behind me. From inside one of the TV station vans I heard a man and a woman calling out answers, or more correctly questions, to "Jeopardy!" Without warning the double glass doors to the county building swung open. Men and women in suits appeared. The media pack moved fast, as if racing for an overdue breakfast, balancing equipment and shouting, "Senator! Senator Watkins!"

Paul Raymer's arms spread wide. He stepped back and up one concrete step, and told everyone to hold their ground. I saw all this from the side.

To the senator's right, and a few feet in front of him, walked Thomas Marquardt, a bow-tied lawyer, sixty-five years of urbane grace under pressure, the best Sacramento representation money could buy. To the left of Watkins was Lee Welty. His right hand held onto the cuff of Watkins' suit coat, as if to steady him. His left hand waved a rolled-up sheet of paper as if it contained revelations. The three of them stopped at the top of the concrete stairs.

Voices barked. Boom microphones shot ahead like lances. Raymer held people back.

Welty's silky talk-show voice called out to the crowd, "The senator has a statement. The senator, has a statement."

I edged up—the giddy mob feeling ran through me the same as everyone—and saw that Watkins was on the sauce again. The pouches beneath his eyes had the sickly yellows, his hair blew like silver straw in the wind. He looked scared.

Marquardt put out both hands, showing his palms. A smile bloomed, a smile that was more professional and less fake than a Lee Welty smile. He answered one of the barking pack: "He pled innocent, because Allan Watkins is innocent."

A gust of wind lifted the senator's tie and wrapped it around his neck.

From the far side of the crowd, to Welty's left, came a question I couldn't hear. Welty turned and said, "We'll answer that." Welty's hair was perfect. His voice was strong even without a microphone. He said, "First, we'll read the senator's statement, then we'll take questions."

Watkins pulled his tie down and tucked it under his buttoned suit coat. This disengaged him from Welty. I flanked the crowd. It saddened me to see Watkins in a weakened state. For all his faults, he loved California and had done more good for its people than almost anyone. I had nothing to lose. I was going to walk right up to him and say I was sure Joe Garston had been murdered. I felt a moment's awareness that what I was about to do was unbalanced, irrational. My emotional involvement in whatever had happened to Joe Garston caused me to leap past common sense. Besides, throwing a wrench into one of Lee Welty's sham performances was too enticing to allow rationality to impede.

Welty swiveled back, to read the senator's statement to the cameras, and his cheek hit a boom microphone that had followed him left. His aviator glasses sailed. Welty looked like he'd just been slapped. He grinned falsely, a kind of broad rictus grin, said, "Excuse me for a moment," and went to retrieve the glasses. Everybody waited for events to return to their scripted format—everybody except a photographer for the scandal sheet *Capitol Roundup*, a short wiry quarrelsome guy named Bob Gruel who I had kicked out of more than a few private gatherings. Gruel slipped by Raymer and started snapping close-ups. Thomas Marquardt, who'd just given a cool aside to the woman reporter wearing a bold red blazer, calmly stepped down and steered the pushy photographer backwards toward the crowd.

Gruel swung his camera in mock threat, and then Paul Raymer made a mistake. He grabbed Bob Gruel from behind. Gruel spun away, screaming. His camera popped Welty in the groin; Welty curled forward, dropped the glasses he had just retrieved, and grabbed his balls. There were shouts and the sounds of scuffling feet. Two deputies, who had been standing away from the speakers and throng, just observing, moved to stop things. In seconds there was a churning pile. Gruel battled them all. He received assistance from some locals, including the Peterbilt cap fellow I'd spoken with minutes earlier. Cameras and iPhones broadcasted everything live on TV and social media.

I ran up the side stairs and said to Watkins, "Your car. This way." I tugged his arm. "Senator!" I implored him above the escalating tumult that was half a dozen concrete stairs below us. When Watkins looked at me, his frowning face showed confusion and booze. For a second, the two of us were separate from all of it. I yanked hard on his coat sleeve. "This way," I repeated. I pulled him behind me.

Thomas Marquardt was looking down at the roiling bodies, half of them fighting, half of them trying to stop the fighting. He shouted someone's name, I think Paul Raymer's, telling him to stop. I saw all this looking back while moving away, then saw Marquardt turn and see me and a moving Watkins. His mouth fell open as I hustled Senator Watkins down the side stairs. Our faces pushed through briny wind.

Behind us Marquardt shouted, "You there! Stop!"

Neither myself nor the former dairy farmer-turned politician stopped. We squeezed between TV vans. The senator's legs kept moving and I steered him to my Jetta and packed him in the back seat. I raced around the front and hopped in, turning the key as the door slammed. We jumped a curb. I saw trees, skidded left. Paul Raymer's hammering fist cracked the back windshield. I swerved left again, avoiding another tree. In the side mirror I caught sight of Raymer rolling away over dry grass. I weaved through mossy coastal pines. Without thinking I leaned on my horn and turned right onto the coast highway, with just enough space ahead of a car where the driver had to hit the brakes fast.

Buildings flitted by, chunks of gray sky, trees, and then hills coated with yellow September grass. I kept my eyes on the road and burned tires through a curve.

From the back seat, Watkins said, "I thought we fired you."

"You did. I'm working for Kate Garston now."

He said, "I don't understand."

"I want to ask you some questions, that's all."

We sailed north. I checked the rear-view mirror, saw the senator rake back wispy hair.

Watkins said, "Wait, you're working for the Garstons? I'll be go-to-hell goddamned." He laughed. It came out of his chest like gravel being crunched, like it hurt. He cleared his throat roughly. "This world gets crazier every goddamn day."

"I saw a chance to get you to talk. I won't have another. Sorry if

I blew your press conference, but I think it was about over anyway."

I glanced in the mirror again. Watkins broke into a spectral smile.

"You're sorry? Hell, son, you were just in time. The vultures were about to eat me on live TV. I wasn't ready for them today." He cleared his throat again. "I still don't know what you think you're pulling, but you saved my hide. Now I get to look like the victim instead of the perp."

I checked the rear-view mirror for cops. I was determined to speak with the senator at length before getting hauled in. The ocean appeared on our left, then the highway curved back and took us inland, under dark redwood trees that sprouted from the ground before the Civil War. My tires barely held the road.

I slowed behind a line of cars. I pulled out left but had to cut back in. The curvy highway made it impossible to pass. My next glance in the mirror yielded a flash of Watkins drinking from a pint of Korbel brandy.

"I've been looking into things. I don't have any proof yet, but—"

"—I want you to drive. Just drive."

I said, "Not a problem. But Senator, I'm trying to tell you I've discovered some unusual things in your case. Extremely unusual."

"If you wouldn't mind," he said, "I'd rather you just drove your damn little car for a while, and we don't talk. I've been talking for forty years. For the time being, I'd appreciate a little rest from it."

I saw Watkins gaze out at a blue cove. The road dipped, crossing a creek that ran under the highway through a culvert. We came out of a turn, rose and passed under flitting tree shadows. I turned right at the next road, a dirt one. We climbed to where the road went sharply right and followed it, paralleling the unseen highway below. The senator never asked where we were going. He bounced around in back, dark bottle poised, lost in thought. When I cut the engine, he blinked with surprise.

We were near the large cypress tree where my notebook had been stolen. Watkins relished a hit of brandy, and screwed the cap back on. He looked at the cap as he secured it, as though this were an act requiring concentration.

He said, "I thought I told you to drive."

I didn't respond.

Watkins took off his tie and jammed it in a pocket of his dark Brooks Brothers suit coat. I saw sweat on his brow. Watkins laughed again, but this time it was higher, and seemed forced. He said, "What, exactly, do you want?"

I told him to get out and sit under the tree. He hesitated, looked at me, then lumbered out of the car and sat with his back against the thick cypress trunk. Out of sight, below the hillside thicket, which was also out of seeing range, a car raced by. Watkins started to speak but I told him to listen. I told him about sitting where he now sat, making notes about the case, hearing noises on the road and following what turned out to be deer through darkness for a couple of hundred feet.

"When I came back," I said, "somebody had stolen my notebook. See? Things are going on here that have nothing to do with your driving."

Watkins thought this over. He nodded and rubbed his cheeks. He went to uncap the brandy, decided not to, and stuffed it in the same bulging pocket as his tie. His rummy face had plenty of heat. "How many votes does that get me on November the fifth?"

I said, "The election's your concern. I want to know who killed Joe Garston."

Watkins reached for the booze, had a snort. Wrinkles charted his face. He mumbled words I missed.

I went to the glove box of my car and removed the chunk of splintered glass held together by a Korbel Brandy label that Sheriff Niles had given me. Watkins watched me with a half-aware detachment. I sat across from him. I took his right hand—the pint of brandy was in his left—and deposited the label and glued glass in it.

Watkins looked at it, registered what it was. He threw it away fast, like you would a lighted cherry bomb. He stared at me with a sagging, pallid face. He gave away nothing. He was like a poker player who preferred to let his opponents reveal their cards first.

I said, "This was in the rocks across the road from where you hit Garston. I got it from Sheriff Niles. He thinks you might find it familiar."

"Who cares what he thinks?" Watkins grinned crookedly. He saluted me with the bottle and took a sip. "What difference does it make?"

"The difference it makes is, it doesn't do you any good to bullshit me. I think somebody threw Garston in front of your car, and I'm going to find out who. I'm going to find out the truth whether you like it or not."

His old-bird white eyebrows rose. I was pushing him. It brought out the fight still stirring in the senator's gut. Taking in breath, he seemed to swell. He rose to his feet. It was the first time I noticed he wasn't much shorter than me.

The senator marched one way, turned and marched back. "You want *truth*? The truth is I've pretty much had the world in the palm of my hand for forty years. I've been lucky, and the well finally ran dry. There's your truth. I wasn't cut out to be a dairy farmer, like my dad. He loved the whole thing." Watkins waved an arm up over his head. "The truth is, I was in the right place at the right time."

Pacing, Watkins spoke as though to a full auditorium. He summarized his life. A childhood on the farm, four years at the University of Nevada, Reno, then back to cows and hay fields. He and his father built a home on pasture the summer he married Marci. He set about repeating his parents' life. It hadn't as yet occurred to him there was an alternative. For eight years he wallowed in mucky grass, in barns, on his back coaxing to life tractor engines that should have been replaced about the time Armstrong stepped on the moon.

Watkins said, "Out of nowhere, Jake Seward dies. He was pumping hands at the American Legion hall down in Cottonwood, and he had a heart attack. I was conceited enough to take a shot at his seat in the state senate."

Watkins described the exhilaration of being thirty, the youngest member of the mammoth California legislature, packing a Ford station wagon and driving his family to Sacramento. He could see pearly snow on the Sierra Nevada a hundred miles east. He felt change running through his veins, and knew it was part of a great wave of change rolling across America. The 1970s were over, a low era of American politics, domestically and in foreign affairs, most notably with Watergate and the miserable end of the Vietnam war. Watkins remembered quite distinctly, he said, the moment it hit him that he would be participate in whatever new directions California and the nation would travel.

The senator stopped walking, caught breath, hoisted the dark slacks over his liquor gut and resumed marching. A siren whirred below, making me jump. Watkins seemed not to hear it. He reached in his coat pocket, pulled out the tie, saw it wasn't brandy and put it back. He paced faster, swinging his arms, and talked about how big California is, in miles and in the mind. He quoted annual yields of cotton, beef, tomatoes, olives and pears. He described a morning on horseback, riding amidst a vineyard near Napa, the grapes so ripe they looked like a million jewels under sunlight. Watkins described standing inside a ring of pink clouds atop Mount Shasta; a silent sunset in the desert; walking the streets of downtown Los Angeles on a warm summer night and feeling, for the first time, the allure of southern California.

"It was like finding my other half," he said. "Discovering another part of me I didn't even know existed."

I imagined Watkins stalking back and forth across pale blue carpet in his capitol office, thinking aloud like this, blowing off steam. It obviously did him good, in the same way a noon tennis match might refresh another.

He said, "The state's arteries are clogged now. A population of more than forty million. Too many people wanting too many things. We can't pro*vide* anymore. The saddest part," Senator Watkins added, "is hardly anyone remembers there were years we could've done almost anything. We did some good, but not enough. Not even close."

He veered and leaned against the passenger door of my Jetta. He flicked sweat off his forehead. The more I heard him talk, the more I understood why Watkins had been re-elected again and again. The man had soul.

He hitched up his slacks, walked some more. Watkins said, "The monkeys I got working for me, they Tweet instead of getting in a room with people and looking them in the eye. Hear each other out. Their reality is what's on their phones. They don't see the big picture. These tiny screens everyone lives by, they make it so no one looks at the sky anymore."

He broke into a run of dry coughs.

I went to my car and took out a bottle of mineral water. I uncapped it, let it fizz, handed the bottle to the senator.

White eyebrows rose. "Water? Is this a joke?"

"Drink some and go sit down, sir. I want you to tell me about Friday night again. Start from the beginning, and don't waste time making things up."

The Senator drank in sips, as if he were taking medicine. He walked to the edge of the road and peed. Then he sat under the big cypress and told his story, changing the two gin and tonics to three, adding the pint of brandy he plucked from beneath the driver's seat on the way home. Watkins described driving with the window open, watching the moon. He said he thought about how fun it would be to drive all night, all the way up the coast to Oregon, and then Watkins broke into another sweat, like the first time he told me about that night. His face was white as a blanched almond.

I said, "You're heading north. You must be close to here by now. What happened?"

His coat was smudged with dust. So were his brown Wingtips, as was his face. The tic ripped his left cheek toward the ear. Watkins rubbed it out, then put the hand down for balance.

"Continue, sir."

The sickly yellows returned to his face. He pitched face-forward onto the dirt. He retched, just water.

I stood over him. "Any minute now, the cops are going to find us. They'll haul me away." I squatted and tapped him on the shoulder. "C'mon, get it over with. Tell me about those few minutes. Something might stick out that'll help me find out who threw Garston down the hill."

His hands wrapped around his head. Watkins said, "You're asking too goddamn much."

I said, "If we keep looking at it, some little detail is going to stick out. Tell me everything that comes to mind. Can't you see I'm doing this for your own good?"

He began to whimper, and it floored me. His whimpering brought me with him to the earth's dry grass, twigs and dirt. The senator's pain was different now. The speeches were over. I sat directly in front of him and was looking at the top of his silvery head. He coughed and spat up water.

I said, "What's so bad it makes you throw up? Like the first time you told me this story."

Watkins looked up and squinted as though looking straight into the sun. "Drive me back to the cabin. I'll see to it no charges are brought against you. I can make that happen."

He went to get up. I pressed down on his shoulder, which stopped him from rising.

Watkins said, "I don't hold grudges. Drive me home and I'll handle the law."

Again he went to get up. This time I pushed him down so hard he tipped over, into the grass. He shook his head and took a breath as if regaining his wits.

I said, "We start with you going up Highway One. After last call at The Cove."

Eleven

Wind lifted creaking cypress limbs. A spider web, damp from the night before, held gleaming drops of water and danced like a parachute in the breeze. I pulled Senator Watkins to a sitting position and told him to drink more water and start talking.

I sat a few feet away, to give him room.

When the senator looked at me, it was as though he saw me from afar. He said, "I'm not sure what to do. I can't trust the phony piece of shit—as you called him—I can't trust Welty with anything other than securing votes. I don't trust him as far as I can throw him."

He took a slug of mineral water, belched.

I said, "What about Marquardt? Did you tell him whatever you're going to tell me?"

He shook his head. His face was a mess of twitches and red wrinkles. "I don't know what I'm going to tell you."

"You mean you can't trust Marquardt with the truth?"

"I trust Thomas. It's not that." The tic jerked at his left cheek, two strikes. "Look, Jeff—look, I did something someone like me doesn't do. I'm thinking, because of your age, you might understand. Sometimes young people do things on impulse they wouldn't do if they faced the same circumstances again. Like the way you basically kidnapped me." He grinned the chalky grin.

And then, after nods and some mumbling to himself, Senator Watkins described picking up a hitchhiker. A young woman.

She was walking up the highway, before the road narrowed. She spun around and put out her thumb and moved her body in his approaching headlights in such a way that, almost without knowing it, the senator said, he pulled over. He'd leaned across the seat to open the door; she opened it herself and hopped in.

"She was in this tiny little white skirt. It was like a sex dream. Driving in the dark, no one around, this half-dressed girl getting in the car with a big smile on her face. I asked where she was headed. She grabbed a whole mop of her hair and said, 'I'm going to see a man about a horse.'" Watkins, squinting, stopped to clear his throat. He looked to be in pain. He said, "That's a saying you don't hear anymore. I started to laugh, she started to laugh, and I just drove on up the road."

His face blazed yellow and red.

"This has been spinning in my head for three days. But anyway, I didn't really know how to talk to her, so I offered her the brandy. From that bottle you got a piece of. She took a lot bigger swallow than you'd think, little as she was. Maybe she felt me staring at her. You know, here I am, an old coot driving under moonlight with this wild-looking creature. I was probably staring at her."

The tic pulled, and it was accompanied by blinking spasms that momentarily closed his left eye.

Below, unseen, a big rig groaned through a turn, then roared up the coast highway. I was playing things as cool as I possibly could.

I said, "Don't worry about it. I'm sure I would've checked her out, too."

Watkins said, "I remember looking at the moon. Then thinking about driving up to Oregon. It couldn't have lasted more than a few seconds, me thinking how nice it would be to walk away from everything. But the truth... This is the problem." The tic jerked his cheek, the left eyelid flattened. He belched like he was holding back vomit. "Truth is, I thought about making her do things. Not anything in particular, but I thought I could do stuff to her and she couldn't put up much of a fight, little as she was.

"And then… I'm going to tell you." Watkins' eyes went wide. He seemed more surprised by this than I was. "I put my hand on her leg, and asked for the brandy back. Just to see what she'd do. She looked straight ahead, maybe trying to ignore me. I slid my hand up her skirt and looked at the top of her leg. It was kind of a game, to see when she'd stop me. She starts screaming. I look up and the boy's right there. I'm not sure if he's picking himself up or not, but that's how I saw it. If I hadn't been acting like a dirty old man, I might not have hit him. I could've hit the brakes, swerved, tried something."

Watkins sprawled forward and heaved. He spit up water, then breakfast. He seemed to let it all out of his middle, retching until it tapered off to a series of bodily spasms.

I got up and went to my car. The back windshield had a crack across it like a crystallized lightning bolt. I remembered the sudden *thwack* of Paul Raymer's fist on glass, the glimpse of him rolling to the left as I swerved and just missed a tree. I looked down the road to the chunk of brandy bottle. I thought of how in a moment—a grab of bare leg, a thought that went too far—the senator's career, forty years, had instantly taken a disgraceful turn that could never be erased.

The senator wiped his mouth and sat up. He brushed dirt off his suit jacket. He brushed his slacks. Watkins seemed cleansed by the sweats. He said, "She was out of the car before I was. She was screaming his name, but she didn't touch him. Not that I saw. I grabbed the bottle, got out the car and threw it at the ocean. I went to go check on the boy and it was like I was made of wet cement. I kind of oozed onto the ground. I had to crawl to make it all the way to him. Last I saw her, she was running up the hillside. I guess she went up here, huh? Is that why you brought me here? Is down there," he said, pointing, "is down there where I hit him?"

"Yes, it is."

Watkins sat there for a bit, taking it in the news. I could feel that it hurt him. He said, "I don't see a way out. The boy's dead. The humiliation factor of admitting everything is why I haven't told Marquardt. Or my wife. That's the worst part. It's going to kill her if it becomes known."

The idea of his actions becoming public silenced us. Having confessed to me, now there were two people who could ruin his life, Molly Garston and myself. Senator Watkins looked like he had just escaped from one jail only to enter another, larger compound.

"Senator," I finally said, "what I care about is finding out who pushed Garston onto the highway. Unless it helps me in that regard, I won't repeat anything you've told me. You have my word."

He scoffed at that. "Hell, I'll deny this conversation ever took place. Clint and Welty would dig up enough dirt on you to make your life miserable. As for the girl, I'll deal with her if and when I have to."

"She's Joe Garston's wife. They were separated. I think he telephoned her before he began walking home."

Squirming, his knees were practically rooting into dirt. Watkins said, "His *wife?*"

"That's right. For some reason I haven't found out yet, she was hitchhiking at two o'clock in the morning, going the same direction Joe and you were."

The senator's bleary eyes rolled up and to the right. I thought he might be about to keel over again. Then I realized he was looking at something, turned and saw a Sunset County patrol car rolling toward us. Blue lights flashed without the accompaniment of a siren. The car dipped and rose, crossing a pothole in the dirt road.

Watkins said, "You know what? I did something dumb, but I didn't harm that girl. Not one bit. And I didn't put that boy out there in the middle of the road, either."

We watched the police car approach. Dust drifted in its wake. I made out Sheriff Niles at the wheel.

Watkins said, "I'm going to fight this goddamn thing. I never get re-elected on the basis of good conduct, anyway."

I said nothing, because the idea of Watkins cleaning himself up, maneuvering around what had happened, using his passing the roadside sobriety test, Joe's foul reputation and arrest record, and who knew what with Molly, didn't seem worthy of a response. Besides, I didn't care about any of that. All I cared about was finding who shoved Joe Garston down that hill.

Niles stopped the police car about thirty feet away, in front of the chunk of brandy bottle. His body jiggled as he climbed out; he waddled our way. He took off his hat, smoothed a hand over the graying mat of hair. He put the hat on as he approached the senator and me.

Niles said, "I had a feeling. I had a feeling, and sometimes when you get a feeling you're right, yes?"

Senator Watkins got to his feet.

I'd never been in jail. I was scared.

Niles said, "You all right?"

Watkins said, "Good as can be expected, all things considered."

Niles looked at me. His head wagged back and forth. "Good God in heaven, Taylor. The whole town is a friggin' beehive." Niles couldn't help himself and he chuckled, his shoulders rising and falling like sandbags. He said, "Sorry, senator. It's just them reporters. They're happy as clams this dumbbell did what he did. It's comical to watch 'em. They're looking into cameras and you can tell they're thinkin' this story can move them up to a bigger station. It's like in their heads they're hearing *cha-ching*."

Niles turned to me and his round forehead pulled together. He said, "Okay, I'm going to read you your rights and take you to the can for creating a public nuisance and reckless driving. I won't give you the notoriety of a kidnapping, because there doesn't seem to have been a struggle. If the senator says you made a threat, that changes everything. Now don't you try and run away. Don't you make me go shoot you in the leg."

Niles told me I had the right to remain silent—then cut himself off with, "Do me a favor, would you? Don't call Kate and have her bail you out. You'll be well fed. We can bring in cable TV. I want you to stay put, till Kate's poor mother can bury her son and get away from all this. Yes? That woman never did like Sunset County, but she was of a time when you moved to where your husband was from and you didn't moan about it. Do you understand what I'm telling you?"

I think Niles was as upset as he got. His hands were at his sides and he kept his bulging gray eyes on mine.

Watkins said, "I'm going to go pick up that glass. I shouldn't have littered."

Niles and I watched the dusty backside of Allan Watkins move down the road, toward the blue patrol car.

Watkins called over his shoulder. "It's my fault. I lost control. I got mad and threw it." He squatted, picked up the brown chunk of glass held together by a Korbel Brandy label. He said, almost casually but with authority, "I want you to know I won't hear of having this young man arrested."

Senator Watkins pocketed the chunk of cracked glass.

Niles glanced at me and made a funny face. He whispered, "Does he got all his marbles?"

I said, "He represents the ninth senatorial district of the Golden State."

Niles hissed, "Don't go getting smart-alek with me. I'll lock you up in the dark and make you find the piss hole on your own."

Watkins, heading back, said, "There's no need to arrest him. It won't serve any purpose at all."

Niles said, "Taylor has broken the law. It's my job to take him in. It's simple as that."

Watkins puffed out his chest. His voice got richer. "You should keep in mind that everyone involved in this is under a tremendous amount of strain. As you yourself said, Jeffrey here is working for Kate Garston. He made a mistake, but he hasn't done anything to be taken in and be arrested for. I mean, Sheriff, I left with Jeffrey on my own accord. To avoid that riot that was developing outside your courthouse. He took me out of harm's way. Do I make myself clear on that point?"

Niles put a vise grip on my arm. I felt his breath in my ear. "All right. I'm giving you a freebie. But I'm warning you, keep out of sight until Mrs. Garston is back on a plane for the desert. I've talked to her twice, and she's in more than enough pain already. She don't need you stirring up talk about somebody maybe set Joe up to get hit. Let's just let things simmer down for a while, no?"

Watkins reached us. His hands were in the pockets of his slacks. He looked as calm as if the three of us were finishing up a morning of bird watching.

"Sheriff," he said, "there's no need to get yourself worked up over this." His was the voice of reason. The senator was the man who remained seated while everybody else was yelling fire and running for exits. Watkins said, "I'll have my staff handle matters in town. Right now, I'd like to see my wife. That's what's foremost on my mind."

He turned and walked toward the patrol car.

When the senator was out of earshot, Niles said, "I still say he's screwy. But he saved your ass, at least for now."

Niles waddled after Watkins. They got in the car. Niles turned off the flashing blue lights. The car made a slow U-turn over dead grass, and rolled away. In the passenger seat Allan Watkins rose a hand above his silvery head in a sort of regal, if disheveled, farewell.

Twelve

Ispent the remains of Tuesday morning under the protective reach of the cypress tree. I was in no hurry to go to town or the campground, where I might be recognized and get hassled. I would have liked to drive over to Ukiah for a gab-fest with Molly Wells, but figured I'd better let things settle down rather than defy Niles' order to keep a low profile until Kate Garston's mother buried her son and left the region. In my car was the well-worn copy of *Democracy in America.* I got it, tried to read but thoughts spun on.

I thought about Joe Garston getting a handful of quarters at Art's. Was it correct to assume he'd made a telephone call? It was the only reasonable conclusion to come to. This brought me to Molly Wells. It seemed likely Joe had reached Molly on her cell where she was playing music Friday night. This would have been a little before midnight, and it wasn't until shortly after two that Watkins had picked her up on the coast highway. That would have given her the right amount of time to get to Sunset from, say, Santa Rosa or Petaluma, which have a fair number of nightclubs. But why wasn't she driving her red Bronco? And, more important, why did she run away when Joe got hit?

The only question involving Molly I had answered was whether or not to divulge Allan Watkins' secret. To Kate or to Sheriff Niles. As keeper of the senator's secret I had leverage over Molly, and leverage over the senator, that I wouldn't have if I told Kate or Niles.

It could come in handy with Molly, and Watkins' influence could keep me out of trouble with the law.

The sky cleared. I drove north. I thought about Watkins saying he wanted to just drive, to get away for a while, and decided to do this in his stead. I drove through Mendocino and Fort Bragg without stopping. Awhile later the highway took me inland, into redwoods. Black trunks flitted by. Fog was replaced by filtered sunlight. The wind smelled of late summer, dry woods. I pulled over and called the campground at Garston Creek. I talked the manager into considering my tent and gear collateral, and promised to return in a few days and pay in full.

I was going home. I hadn't even known I missed it: I had to see and smell and taste Grantsville. This need was somehow tied to quitting Sherman Investigations, and with taking a new path. On the way, I spent the night at a motel in Eureka.

The next day I drove through redwood forests for two hours. In spots they thinned into grasslands. The landscape was green, not the yellowish brown of the rest of California from May till November rains. And then I was home. A weaving of deer antlers arched over the one intersection that is downtown Grantsville. Dogs on the street were without metal license tags. The wooden buildings needed paint, but they were sturdy enough.

People anywhere from twenty to seventy years old came to me with outstretched hands. Claire Wright came out of Wright's Market and started laughing, loudly, right there on the old wood sidewalk elevated two feet to accommodate lashing winter rains. She hugged me and looked me over. There was general agreement I was a city slicker.

"Just take a gander," Claire said to her husband, Loren, when he came out wiping his hands on his jeans before shaking my half a right hand without hesitation.

Most everyone had seen the antics of the day before on TV or the internet. Hijacking Senator Watkins was right up the alley for fiercely independent folks like those of Grantsville.

A dozen of us went to Blue Heron Cafe. I ate a free lunch. People dropped by. The place filled and by dinner it got silly with beer and tales, and true stories. A few people asked about my mom, though most everybody knew the same things: she and Del Beverage were in Alaska; Mom worked at a travel agency; Del worked half the year in a fish cannery and drank beer the other half.

When asked what I'd been doing since college, I skimmed over working for Sherman Investigations. I didn't mention choosing not to go to medical school in Seattle, though I'd been accepted. No one pressed me to talk about my hand. The people of Grantsville thought more highly of me than I did, and that was an influence in doing what was right with regard to the death of Joe Garston. It helped me to say to hell with where cards might fall.

I slept at Loren and Claire's. The next day I wandered around town and talked with people I hadn't seen for half a dozen years, or even longer. I hiked the woods I hiked as a boy. I climbed to the top of a redwood tree and perched there, letting the wonders of life, even a half-fouled-up life like mine, sink in. I thought about the sky. From where did its blue come? Where did everything come from? Had I lived before, and if so, where and what had my life been like? What do you do with a life the very nature of which you don't understand?

These were the same questions I'd asked myself during those countless hours alone while a child. These were the questions I had asked while living alone behind the Blue Heron Cafe, seventeen years old, waiting to go to the big city, enter college and play basketball. The questions hadn't left me. I was thankful for that.

Several people in town decided I was on the run from the law. They clung to the idea and wouldn't believe me when I told them that, so far at least, there were no charges. Mac Wilkens even offered to run me up to Canada in his salmon trawler. When I explained to him I was a free man, he said, "Let's do it anyway, for old times' sake."

Mac was on the team that had brought Grantsville its only state championship trophy. He could have gone away and lived a different, what is thought of as a bigger life, but Mac chose not to leave the ancient redwood trees, the lungs-filling air, and the feeling of living in Paradise. Mac was a smart man. We hung out together off and on for three days. I could tell he saw something was eating at me, but he refrained from asking. He'd leave it as my decision whether or not to talk about things.

I didn't make promises to get together with anyone, or exchange email addresses, or any of that. I avoided the peppy chatter I'd used with people in my work for Sherman Investigations. I simply said goodbye to old friends, hugged them and responded to their words with, "I love you, too." The drive back to Sunset County was an arduous haul. By the time I found my tent and sleeping bag, I crawled into the sack and fell into a deep sleep without finishing even one page of *Democracy in America*.

I had a disturbing dream. In it a spirit stood above me and to the right. It was neither male nor female. It was faceless, without features, and was made of millions of curling, electrically charged gold threads. The figure bent toward me. I tried to cry out, but no sound came. I was terrified. When I tried to roll away from it, I couldn't move. Then I saw that the spirit was making a kind of offering. It extended a bouquet of sparking yellow flowers.

The flowers dropped on my chest. Electricity surged through me. I tried to knock the bouquet off me but was unable to move. The buzzing electric current was holding me hostage when I heard:

".... gone! B-B's gone, Jeff. He was gone when I got home about an hour ago."

Twitching with electricity, I awoke. I saw Kate Garston's face among tumbling dark hair. Hunched over in my low dome tent, she yanked at the side of my sleeping bag.

Kate said, "I think B-B ran away."

Thirteen

Kate said, "They told me at Greenwood they thought you went here."

Brushing by a hunched-over Kate, I scrambled out of my sleeping bag and then out of the blue dome tent. I stood in a sea of tents and other people's camping gear, wearing underwear and a gray sweatshirt, shaking off the electrically charged dream.

Kate stepped to across from me. She said, "I don't want to go back there alone."

I kept my head down, so I didn't have to look into her waxy eyes, the pinched dark face. "What makes you think I have any idea what you're talking about?"

I still saw flashes of sparking yellow-gold electric threads, and the faceless figure leaning toward me.

Kate said, "Of course you don't know. But I can't stop it from coming out."

To my right a young father cooked oatmeal over a popping campfire. His two daughters ran back and forth to a white Volvo station wagon for kitchen items; the car doors were left open like cupboards. I looked up. I saw sunlight pushing through mist. I risked a look at Kate. Her eyes were wide, bright.

I said, "What time is it?"

"A little after ten. My mom took the first flight out of Santa Rosa at six-thirty. I dropped her off and came straight back."

I shivered. I had driven all of the day and most of the night before, stoked by thoughts of rolling into Sunset, solving the mystery of Joe Garston's death and leaving town a hero. I admit there were scenes of Kate and me in these fantasies. She had been a writhing, cooing lover in my mind. In the flesh she was more loopy than sexy. Her gaze stayed about a foot above my head, as if she were looking at someone behind me.

I said, "Okay. From the beginning."

She took the Camels out of her back pocket. I declined her offer, watched her light up. "When I got back from the airport," Kate said, "B-B was gone. He must have waited for me to leave this morning, packed up his stuff and split." She took a puff, squinted against rising smoke. Her hand jittered. "B-B's been living in the old bunk house for years. He put a microwave and hot plate out there."

"Does he always keep you apprised as to his whereabouts? Maybe he waited till after the funeral to go away for a spell. He could be more upset about Joe than he lets on."

Kate spoke to that unseen person behind me. "He's upset about Joe all right. Me, Mom and B-B are probably the only people who are. But he's gone. I looked in the bunkhouse. It's obvious he left us."

The *us* didn't make literal sense to me, but I let it sail by. "For the sake of discussion, what difference does it make if Stiving leaves and doesn't come back?"

Kate looked like the question was beyond her range of comprehension. "He's never done anything like this before."

"I understand. But what difference does it make if he leaves? I need to know things like this if I'm going to be able to help you."

Kate looked down. She picked a thread of tobacco from her lips. She was shaking a little all over as she said, "B-B was not a slave. But he's loyal." She puffed, looked up. "He knows the grunt side of logging better than I do. He kept an eye on things for me. If B-B split, something's wrong. Something bad is wrong."

To my left the engine of a Winnebago, twenty thousand pounds of home away from home, began its low thrumming warm-up idle. Black smoke spread. I said, "I have an idea. Why don't you tell me what you wanted to tell me when you came. We'll start from there. We can get into loyalty stuff later."

Kate ground out her cigarette in the palm of her left hand, and tucked it into a front pocket of her jeans. She said, "I want you to come with me to the ranch, to help me go through his things. What's left of them. He's been jumpy as hell lately. Even before Joe got hit. Now he's gone. I want to know why."

"If he had anything to hide, he probably wouldn't leave it, don't you think?"

Kate said, "We still got to try." She worked fingertips into the front pockets of her tight jeans. "Look, I want you to go with me because I'm freaked about being up there without anybody else around. Okay?"

She walked to her pickup truck, the Ford half-ton of no discernible color, and waited while I went into the tent and put on jeans and shoes and socks. The woman had paid me. It was time to go to work.

Following her up Garston Ranch Road, we broke through mist into sunlight. Ahead was the timeworn white farmhouse with a columned, lopsided front porch, the carriage and bunkhouses, and rotting pump-house. The buildings were checkered with wide cracks in their dull white paint. With a rusted tractor and scything equipment to one side of the house, and a rotting oxcart sunk half a foot into the ground on the other side, the Garston spread looked more like a stop on a tour of old West ghost towns than a place where people lived.

Kate didn't slow at nearing home. Her tires spit gravel and her truck bucked when halting. I stopped my Jetta, which seemed like a bantam toy next to her large dirty truck. Once we were inside, Kate transferred mounds of business papers from one end of a scarred redwood slab table—the table probably seated twelve—to the other. She had me sit while she prepared breakfast. We ate scrambled eggs, bacon and toast, and made small talk about the beauties of the ridge, about how the sky seemed to wrap around the homestead like a blue shawl. It was clear to me that she was glad for the company. After we put our dishes in the kitchen sink, Kate led me through a side door, across an unkempt garden, to the former bunkhouse.

B-B Stiving's quarters smelled like the wad of money Kate had given me, only the mustiness was more fulsome. However, the place was not a dump. It was the cluttered home of a bachelor. I'd never searched through anyone's private belongings and wasn't keen on doing so. Kate went right to a pine dresser and slid open a drawer.

I said, "What are you looking for?"

"Anything that might have to do with Joe. Anything." There was an assumed authority to her voice, like that of a Mother Superior searching the convent dormitory for cosmetics and romance novels. There were empty patches on the floor, lighter and defined by rectangles of dust, though I couldn't guess what B-B might have taken. A green Hefty bag was stuffed with crushed beer cans. The one stab at décor he'd made was to staple empty rice sacks onto one wall, making a pattern of Chinese writing in bold strokes of red and blue. Kate pulled them off the wall, one at a time, and reached inside them. Her lack of hesitation, her sense of ownership, held an eerie quality, as if B-B Stiving, though he'd lived there for years, didn't fully exist.

I climbed a steep ladder to the loft, which was the same rectangle as the first floor. A square window let in feeble light. A cord was tacked along the outside of the ladder and it went up the wall next to me and then to the middle of the ceiling, where there was a fixture of a bare bulb and a string hanging down. I pulled on the string and cracked my shin on something.

My swearing brought Kate to the bottom of the ladder. "You all right?"

"Not a problem. I just didn't see all this stuff on the floor."

Kate said, "I'm surprised he left those."

I looked around, my eyes adjusting to the light, and saw what at first looked like giant spiders. Then I saw they were redwood burl, one carved into an octopus, another into a large fish. A few had deer heads adorned with antlers scored into them.

I said, "Don't tell me the guy who beat the crap out of me made these." I rubbed my shin. "He didn't seem the artistic type."

Kate said, "He was always working on something." Her voice carried up the ladder, through the opening, into the now-lighted chamber. "He'd pull out old stumps and make things. He even sold some to people who have vacation homes around here. Gil Johnson got him started. You heard of Gil Johnson? He's pretty famous in the city."

I told her I had not heard of Gil Johnson.

Kate called up, "It's kind of odd he left those. He knew I was going to Santa Rosa. He had the time to take 'em. See that door?"

I hadn't, but I did now, a redwood door that opened into air. Next to it was coiled rope and a block-and-tackle set up. I said, "Yeah?"

"He had plenty of time to lower those into the back of his truck. Maybe he's not really leaving."

It hit me like a shot: I loved the rise and fall of Kate's voice. It seemed a natural part of the landscape, a landscape like that of my childhood, and that lush forest that began a hundred yards behind her house. And I was as glad for the company as she was. I was standing in a large room atop another large rectangular room when I realized Kate Garston reminded me of my mother.

I heard her rummaging through things below.

My head sank, nodding, remembering Mom's voice and that she was about the same age as Kate now was when she ran off with Del Beverage. I got hot all of a sudden, stood and looked at shelves built into the walls, shelves that held rags and carving tools, cans of clear Watco oil. What a fire hazard, I thought. There was no ventilation. That was a problem. I went to the window and with effort slid it open a few inches. I began looking for clues as to why Bobby Stiving had split. Anything to avoid thinking about emotional connections between Kate Garston and my mother.

I pulled the string, cutting the light, and made my way to the ladder. I backed down it. I told myself to forget about the peculiar thought. I turned around. I lost my breath.

In Kate's right hand was a large pistol. It was in front of her face, pointing sideways. Slowly, gently, she ran her tongue along the glinting barrel. Then she pressed her lips to it. Through a window behind her came a block of whitish sunlight. Kate was surrounded by a halo of glittery dust.

"Kate! Kate! What the—?"

She flinched. The pistol blew a hole in the ceiling.

Kate screamed and turned, swinging the pistol. Red and black splotches swam in front of me. My legs buckled; I sank to the floor. I heard panting, my own.

Kate, her voice cool and utterly dry, said, "Now we'll never know."

She looked at the gun in her hand. The twinkle in her brown eyes drove a quiver down my spine.

"Never know what?"

I watched glittery dust motes swirl all around her. It was hypnotizing.

Kate said, "If it's been fired in the last day or two, there's a trace of gunpowder you can taste. It could be anywhere on the barrel. I was just, just—hey. You don't think… You didn't think I was going to…"

"I hadn't gotten that far."

My vision was still splotchy. My head burned with heat.

She curled dark hair around an ear, frowned. Kate spoke to her feet. "I was just checking it before we took it to the cops. I was going to have them do a test. I was curious. But now I guess we can't."

As a kid I shot a deer, and in high school, after a six-pack, we'd go waste possums. I'd been pretty good with guns, but a large part of me had always hated and feared them and once I moved from where I'd used them in order to be accepted by my peers, I'd never touched one. Or wanted to. I went to Kate and took this one from her hand. I put it on a counter beside dirty dishes, with the barrel pointed toward the wall. Then I plopped into an old brown bean bag chair.

Kate sat on the bed. "It's a good thing there's not a water tank up there anymore. Before electricity, that's where the water for the house was stored." She pointed at the bullet hole in the ceiling. "We'd be drenched by now."

She smiled giddily. "You got to admit, that's funny."

I said, "Yeah, a real knee slapper."

Kate said, "Let's go check Joe's place."

She put out a hand and pulled me to my feet. She shut the door behind us. We walked along a concrete path that had sunk and cracked with age. Kate told me that Joe had moved out of the main house when he was still a teenager. The final blow with their parents came when he was busted for having pot on the front seat of his truck, right in plain view while parked in downtown Sunset. He'd taken up residence in the old carriage house and their parents were fine with the distance. Joe lived there until he married Molly, about five years before. When he and Molly had wearied of brawling and separated, Joe moved back into his old place.

"He just got worse after that," Kate said.

The inside of the carriage house was somewhat like Stiving's place, only there was a kitchen and dining area. Kate began going through Joe's stuff. It made me feel creepy. She handed me an empty wooden fruit crate. She slid open a desk drawer and tossed papers into the box I held—torn envelopes, what looked like court documents—without giving them more than a glance. I found a cardboard box filled with kindling for burning in the wood stove, emptied it, knocked out the dust and brought it to Kate. She sat on her knees going through a pine dresser.

She filled the box, plus another fruit crate. We walked back along cracked concrete, past the bunk house and sinking oxcart and weedy garden.

Kate said, "What's odd is, that gun was Joe's. Unless he gave it to B-B for a debt. It belonged to our grandfather. Did you notice it was a Colt 45?"

"I was too scared to notice much of anything."

Kate said, "I just wonder how it got over to B-B's. If Joe gave it to him, it must have been for a debt."

We dumped the booty onto the kitchen table. Sifting through it, Kate said, "I don't know if we'll find anything. It's mostly junk. Some old letters from Molly. Lots of printouts from the sheriff's department."

"Did your brother leave a will?"

Kate divided a pile of papers into two. "There's no way he had a will. Joe was the most disorganized person in the world."

Kate told me to leave the last box full; there was no more room on the table. She said, "I might as well look through it all myself first." She lit a cigarette, brought over a glass ashtray. "Make yourself at home. I'll make a pile of anything we might look into, but my guess is we're basically cleaning house."

I went to the front parlor. Pine bookshelves were built into one of the wooden walls. There was a gold-leafed set of Dickens, works by Wallace Stegner, Bernard De Voto, George R. Stewart and other chroniclers of America's westward expansion and settlement. Also fiction by Tolstoy, Mark Twain, Willa Cather and Hemingway; few of the novels were published after the Second World War. There was no TV. I read by the light of a table lamp—the wagon-wheel chandelier loomed above—but kept changing books and wondering what Kate was up to. I finally went to the kitchen to make a late lunch.

Kate, seated at the large redwood slab table, wore reading glasses. Upon seeing me she took them off. She blew away a strand of frizzy brown hair.

Kate said, "It's hard to think any of this stuff could be important to anybody. Let's face it, Joe's life was sad as hell."

I made ham sandwiches, and found Cokes in the refrigerator. We ate in silence. I went back to the parlor, couldn't read, and told Kate I was going for a walk. Just before entering the woods I passed a wrought-iron fence that enclosed the family cemetery, with gravestones dating back to the early 1900s. Joe's was there. A fresh gray marble headstone listed his years. I wondered how many people showed up to see him off.

I followed a trail downhill through redwoods. I reached a creek. Green and gray pebbles were magnified in clear water. I splashed my face and sat. It felt weird knowing my mind made a connection between Kate and Mom. I decided it was just one of those fleeting thoughts, say of screwing the hot bank teller after she gets off work, that sometimes flash through you, never to be heard from again.

When I returned to the house, Kate quit reading Joe's papers. She brought me a beer and we sat in the parlor.

She told me she had found a few items among Joe's things she didn't recognize, and said she'd try to track them down. "Doing this has woken me up. I mean, I haven't started all the legal stuff, for Joe's death."

We continued with small talk over another round of beer. A mile to the west, the lighthouse rose like a white finger through incoming clouds. Somehow, we started talking about the books I'd looked through. She showed me a few of her favorites. She wore a wheat-colored sweater. Her feet were bare under the snug jeans. By the time we were eating Brio crackers and Jack cheese, I was stationed with my feet up on an arm of the faded pink Tudor chair I'd sat in the first time I stepped into that room.

Kate sat on the brown couch. She smirked, slyly. "I've been waiting for you to tell me about your adventure with Allan Watkins."

I told her everything except what was most important: Watkins picking up Molly Wells. I felt, at least for now, it was right to keep that to myself. As far as I knew, he was guilty of poor judgment, but no true negligence or malice.

Far off, the sun dipped behind advancing clouds, which were low and turning purple. Kate flicked on the chandelier. The telephone rang.

She went around the corner to the black telephone in the hall. "Hello." A second later she said, "Hi, Cliff. What's up?"

It was quiet for a bit, until Kate said, "Oh." A few seconds later: "God, I'm so sorry. That's awful."

Next, she said, "I haven't seen him all day. He was gone when I came back from taking my mom to the airport. And it looks like he's moved out."

A full minute passed with her listening. By then I was on my feet, though I stayed in the parlor.

Finally, Kate said, "You sure it was his truck? Couldn't Anderson be wrong?" Another minute of listening. Then she said, "Actually, he's here."

I went to the wooden archway that led to the entrance hall. Kate was bent forward, facing the wall. She said, "He told me about the notebook a while ago."

Her left hand fished for cigarettes at the back pockets of her jeans. Kate nodded toward the wall. "I'll give him the message." She found the cigarettes but didn't slip them from her pocket. "Of course I will—Jesus, Cliff, I'm sorry about Doug. Really sorry." Kate hung up. She turned around. I stepped forward. She grabbed my hands and shook them like reins on a horse.

Kate said, "Somebody killed Doug Kolatch. It looks like it might've been B-B."

Fourteen

I took Kate by the arm and escorted her to the parlor. She sat on the couch. Her eyes were so glazed she may as well have been blind. She told me Deputy Kolatch's wife had come home from work and found him face down on the living room floor. He had a bullet in his chest. Neighbors had seen B-B's truck parked at the house in the morning, but nobody heard any shots. And finally, in searching Kolatch's house, Sheriff Niles found my notebook that had been stolen the night I followed deer along the fire road. It was tucked under extra blankets in a closet.

Kate was staring about a foot above my head. I asked if there were anything I could do.

Kate said, "I'd like a scotch and water." She pushed dark hair from her face. "It's in the cabinet above the cutting board. Feel free to make one for yourself."

I headed for the kitchen.

Kate said, "Oh, Cliff says he doesn't want you to leave Sunset County without checking in with him. He needs to keep the notebook, but you can look through it all you want."

I called back to the parlor. "My notebook showing up in his deputy's house might make him more amenable to talking with me."

"Cliff says the place was ransacked. But why would B-B go to Doug's after pulling out of here? And what was Doug doing hiding in the bushes around where you think Joe got pushed through?"

Returning with drinks, I handed Kate a glass and sat at the other end of the couch. I heard the refrigerator humming, two rooms away, a creak in one of the windows, and a crow cawing somewhere outside. Every sound on that ridge was separate, distinct, beautiful and eerie. Like a ghost town.

Kate worked a bit of scotch around on her tongue. She said, "You know, I was still holding out for Joe being drunk, and Watkins being drunk. A part of me was holding out for it, deep down inside." She took another sip, tipped her head back and shook out her hair.

I said, "Now it's just a question of who was involved, and in what way. Don't you think?"

She nodded. She looked dizzy. Kate's voice rose. "God, did B-B really kill Doug? I don't know what to think. I don't want to think about anything right now." She took a bigger swallow of scotch and winced as it went down. Looking around the room, Kate said, "Doug was a handful as a kid, but he moved away to an aunt and uncle's in Sonoma during high school. He came back married, with a degree in criminal justice from Sonoma State, and became a damn good cop. He and B-B ran in different circles now, but when we were kids they used to hang out together. They were good friends till Doug went off to high school down in Sonoma." She took another swallow. "I got to quit talking like this. We really don't know if B-B did it. Someone just says he saw B-B's truck there, that's all."

We let that settle into the dusty corners of the room.

Kate went over to the stereo. She tried getting a classical station on the radio. The reception was fuzzy. She looked wonderful, considering the circumstances. Her beige sweater was new looking and fit her as closely as her jeans. She had smooth skin that was naturally tan from being active outdoors rather than sunbathing. A persistent air of loss traveled with Kate, but under that I thought I sensed an inner richness I never found among the women I met during the three years I worked for Sherman Investigations.

She gave up on music, went to a picture window and pulled the drapes closed. After drawing a second set of drapes shut, Kate let her weight rest against the wall of old wood.

I said, "This morning you drove to Santa Rosa, said goodbye to your mom and drove back. You discovered B-B had cleared out. You went and found me. We searched the rooms, you took a bunch of your brother's personal papers, which probably haven't been a whole lot of fun to look through. You get a call that says somebody you knew, the guy who arrested the senator for hitting your brother, got killed. And B-B's the prime suspect. I mean, it's probably not a bad idea to take some time off. Maybe you could even leave some drapes open. I hate to see you block that view."

Kate had gone to another picture window; she turned. Her hands went to her hips. Her expression was wistful. "That's the one thing that never gets old around here. Looking out at the world. How it changes all year, then it gets like it was all over again."

She came to the couch and finished her scotch. She grabbed cigarettes from the end table, lit one, took a puff, shook out the match. She took another puff and sighed. She stood, had a short third puff, bent and ground out the smoke.

Kate said, "My head's about to burst. You know? Let's get out of here."

We went out the back door. We passed the bunkhouse—I thought of the pistol left on the counter in there—the carriage house, a barn and corrals, and rotting chicken coops. Beyond that the land dropped and we walked to a grassy mesa, where there was a pond. Night was falling fast. A flock of tiny birds wheeled, dipped toward the water, rose in unison and flashed white bellies. They disappeared over dark trees. The pond, roughly a circle of about an acre, was the color of slate. Our feet plunked onto a weathered dock.

I said, "You come here often?"

Kate said, "I used to. Not anymore."

I couldn't make out the lighthouse at the point, but a mile below us cypress and redwood trees lined Highway One. The trees were darker than the sky. Between them blazed sparks from speeding headlights. Somewhere down there, I thought, Joe Garston had been murdered.

We sat on the dock. Water was to both sides of us. Stars sprinkled bits of light across the pond.

Kate said, "When I think about the chaos surrounding my brother's life, it's overwhelming. Going through his papers, it really sinks in. All the crazy business deals. I don't think even one of them was worth a crap."

I was nervous. I think I was nervous because there I was, sexually drawn to Kate and probing about her recently dead brother at the same time. I ran my bad hand over the top of cold pond water.

I said, "Joe never worked for Garston Timber?"

Kate said, "When my parents sold the majority of the business, the idea was I'd manage the new company and Joe would oversee contracts in the field. We thought he could grow into it. He acted like he was ready to straighten up. It just never worked out."

Kate was sitting in a half lotus, looking up. I leaned back on my elbows and thought that if I'd been handed a plate as full as Joe Garston's, I sure as hell would have made it work out. Half owner of thousands of acres of timberland near the California coast, you start out as the boss and end up the town joke? A sad life with a sad ending.

Kate said, "He left debts. He's behind on court-ordered payments for a CD Molly cut in L.A. He owed some stores in town. But none of those are too bad. Then I come across a piece of paper, a handwritten IOU. Ten thousand dollars to Ed Lantis, signed by both of 'em. Dated August seventeen. Ten thousand bucks! I don't know why Ed would let Joe go into debt to him without telling me. He's an old friend of the family."

"It's my understanding you and Ed Lantis used to be more than friends."

I listened to unseen doves. The night was dark, the sky clear, the stars bright. Kate stretched out on her side and faced the pond.

She said, "I see the rumor mill's been busy." Her words were directed over the water. "Ed and I were together when George Bush was president, for God's sake. Did they cart out Gil Johnson, too?"

"The name, but not in that context. And 'they' was Sheriff Niles. I asked him about you when I was working for Senator Watkins. Niles told me you and Lantis were once a couple. He also said you sometimes hang out with 'the artsy fartsy crowd.' I gather Johnson is a leader in that group."

Kate snorted a laugh. I looked at her backside, the long wiry frame. My hand went to her shoulder. An inch before touching her, I reeled it back.

Kate said, "Look, Jeff, Ed Lantis and I are the last two sizeable independents in this part of the state. Sometimes we double up on bids and try to beat the corpos." Sighing, she rolled onto her back. Toward me. She was right next to me. Kate said, "I guess you heard that when I was a freshman at Davis, Ed and I said we were going to get married."

"That's the one."

"Well," Kate said, "what happened was, after I was home for Easter break my period didn't come. So we told our parents we'd decided to get married. We were going to act like we couldn't take being so far apart—Ed was here working for his folks. The plan was to act like I got pregnant after we decided to get hitched."

Quail made chugging sounds in the grass; rising, their wings fluttered in the cool dark air. Kate looked at me and smiled. It was a tired smile. Still on her back, Kate put her knees up. I saw the outline of her face. The night smelled of the pond water and dead grass.

She said, "By the time school was out, I wasn't sure I wanted to go through with it. I did something I think was pretty smart for a dumb nineteen-year-old. One day when Ed came over, I was shoveling shit in the stables. We still had horses then. He tells me I shouldn't be doing any manual labor. 'Not in your condition,' he said. He said, 'Not in your condition,' until I got sick of it and put the shovel down. We walked down here to wash off. We swam to where the water shoots in from the pump, over there. I let it hit my stomach. To see what it felt like." Kate lifted her head from the dock. "Do you think it's odd I'm telling you all this?"

"What I think is odd is what most people think is normal."

Kate said, "I was sick of hearing I had to be taken care of. So I told him to get ready, because I had something important to tell him. I had to talk loud to be heard over the pump and the water. I told Ed I'd driven down to Santa Rosa and had an abortion."

Though there were no tears, that the words mattered to her was made clear by the way her voice cracked.

Kate said, "I was testing him. See?"

"How'd he do?"

"After a whole five seconds, he told me I'd done the right thing. No, he said 'the best thing.' He said a baby could mess up our relationship. That he wasn't going to get stuck in the timber business because we were going to move to New Mexico, and he was going to build adobe houses. We were kids, you know? The more he talked the more it was already over. I broke up with him like two weeks later."

She rolled toward me. Our faces nearly touched.

I said, "Do you still hate him for it?"

"No, it *was* the best thing. After we broke up, I told my parents I was going to visit a dorm friend in Davis. I drove to Sacramento, used a fake name, and had one. It's still the hardest thing I've ever done." She closed her eyes for a few seconds. She opened them. Kate said, "Okay, I still hate him, but you learn to live with it."

I kissed her, to stop the flow of painful words.

She ran a hand down my cheek, looked me in the eyes.

I said, "I want to be honest with you. I don't know how or what I feel."

Kate took my face in both of her hands and kissed me. Her lips were warm, full. I tasted Scotch and tobacco. She was both pulling me to her and pushing her mouth hard against mine. Her tongue darted. I wrapped my arms around her and we rolled back and forth across the dock. I put a hand under her sweater. The way she moved under me—and the cooing sound that passed from her mouth into mine—made her even lovelier than I had imagined.

Kate rolled us over; we almost took a dunking. We rolled back to the middle of the dock. The night was clear and without wind. The zipper of her jeans ripping open sounded like a promise. Her jeans hadn't reached her knees and my hand was in her lush dark wetness. I don't know how much she took down my pants and how much I did, but I quickly felt fresh air on the back of me.

Her calls had a hoarse, desperate quality that urged me on and on and on. For a while I lost all sense of where I was. My eyes were open, but they didn't see anything. I was grinding myself into a dome of pure pleasure. I heard Kate's bones hitting the dock planks. I rose, slowing our rhythm so as not to hurt her. She rose and slapped her hips against mine. Down I went.

I'd been straightforward when I told Kate I wasn't sure how I felt toward her. I did know one thing: Being with Kate sparked a fire in me regarding missing my mom that I'd tamped down for ten years. My best friend had left me, and it had hurt so much I hadn't wholly felt it till Kate reawakened that part of my past. Even knowing that, it didn't feel depraved being with Kate. It didn't feel warped to be intimate with her. It felt more like going home.

PART TWO

Fifteen

I spent the night in an old army sleeping bag on a downstairs couch. In the morning I climbed the wooden stairs and we made love in Kate's bed. She had a couple of bruises on her behind from the dock the night before. I had one on the inside of my right forearm. Neither of us mentioned them while we rested, after. We didn't speak. Kate didn't smoke. We began again and I released years of suppressed love, desire, and I'm sorry to say, anger. I can accurately use these words now, but in the moment it was pure dizzying sensations. It was as if I were drilling years of unacknowledged feelings into Kate's center. She thrust back into me with equal intensity.

We took our first shower together. We had lunch, lounged around, then I got dressed and drove to Sunset. I was going to have a look at my notebook. What I had written in it was not of interest—nothing to learn there. I was interested to see if Doug Kolatch, or anyone else, had added notes of his or her own. Or if there were underlines, say, or a circle drawn around one of the names—anything beyond what I had recorded.

I parked outside the county complex of redwood buildings. Both the Stars and Stripes and the California Bear flag flew at half staff. I went to the sheriff's office. Desk clerk Anne Simpson was on shift. She said hello in her unaffected park ranger's voice, though it didn't take great powers of observation to see a dullness to her skin, and hear sadness beneath her greeting.

125

I said, "It's horrible about Doug Kolatch. It's a total shock."

Anne looked to the counter. She said, "Oh, did you meet him? During your goings on this past week?"

"No... I'm... sorry."

I felt heat on my cheeks. I was blushing because of the morning's romps with Kate, and the complicating mental presence of my mother, and all of it made me feel like a pervert in the presence of Anne's forthright earnestness and grief.

I said, "Please forgive me for getting to business, but I'm here to look through my notebook found at Kolatch's. Is the Sheriff available? He says I can look at it."

Anne said, "He's not here right now. We don't expect him in today unless an emergency comes up. He's on shift tomorrow. Filling in for Doug."

Anne went to the same locked drawer where she had deposited the ten thousand dollars in cash for Allan Watkins' bail. She opened it and took out the little notebook. This time I signed a kind of check-out slip, even though I wasn't allowed to take the notebook out of her sight. There was a stool at the right end of the chest-high counter. I sat and opened the spiral notebook. I looked at the pages while talking with Anne.

I said, "How's your investigation going? The one on your own time."

Anne said, "Right now my investigation involves getting you to tell me about your investigation."

I said, "Doesn't sound like you've found very much."

"And you?"

I could have told Anne about Watkins picking up Molly while driving north, just short of where Joe got hit, but I was keeping that for Niles. It wasn't an apple fritter, but I'd save the information as an agreeable present to him. I said, "I'm still basically in the dark."

Anne had stayed at her station, maybe ten feet to my left, on the other side of the tall counter. "That was wild, by the way, you

126

scooping Watkins away from his press conference. Nobody here likes him, so we all thought it was pretty cool."

I shrugged. I enjoyed Anne. She was completely no bullshit.

Anne said, "Are you going to Bodega Bay tonight?"

"Excuse me?"

Anne said, "Are you going to The Tides restaurant? The Wellbeats are playing there every weekend in September."

"You're a step ahead of me. Are you going?"

Anne said, "I can't. That's why I told you about it. We have our weekend-after-Labor-Day family reunion. I'm going straight there from here."

No matter how much we talked, Doug Kolatch's murder still claimed most of the air in the room. Our interactions were stilted. Plus I didn't have the desire to play-chat with Anne like I had before. I got back to business and looked through my notebook. Anne answered a question on the dispatch radio. A couple of people entered and asked for directions. I smelled the notebook. I held it up to the light and searched it. Nothing. I returned it to Anne. Before she put it away, when I said thank you, without thinking I offered my right hand, which created another stilted moment.

She set the notebook on the counter and shook my hook. It was like she didn't know what else she could do.

I said, "Now I'm the one who feels stupid."

She said, "No worries. Come back tomorrow if you want to talk to Cliff."

I said goodbye. Anne said good luck.

I drove to the campground, gathered my gear and left money in the pay slot on the way out. I wandered around town. I looked at real estate offerings in windows, shocked at what a place as far away from city amenities as Sunset went for. I chalked it up to the millions of seniors you see everywhere now, the gray armies, who can sell their paid-for homes and retire to most anywhere they choose. Next I went to the beach and spent an hour looking at the sea. When it came time to eat, I skipped The Cove and Art's and went to Perry's, the town deli. That way I wouldn't have to talk about Joe Garston and or Senator Allan Watkins with anyone. I called Kate's cell and left a message telling her where I was going.

With the sun dropping behind the sea, I drove south for ninety miles. Entering The Tides, I saw a Wellbeats poster with the dates they'd play there listed. I arrived late in the first set, sat near the back and ordered a bottle of Anchor Steam beer. The music was mainly variations on the I-got-drunk-and-lost-love theme. I could barely view diminutive Molly Wells singing her woes into a microphone, but I have to say her voice caught in all the proper places. And when the cowpokes raced their guitars she spun around that portable stage like a whirligig. Her brassy hair snapped the air like a whipping flag.

On a napkin I drew a north-south line. Left of the line I wrote OCEAN. To the right I wrote 2 A.M. HITCHHIKER.

I gave the waitress a twenty and asked her to slip the folded note to Molly. During the second set I moved closer to the stage. It didn't take her long to spot me. I gave Molly a surreptitious wave. Thereafter I could tell she was going through the motions with the music. At midnight, when the show ended, I moved to a corner table.

Guys unplugged equipment and took it out a side door.

Molly went to the bar for a drink. People came by, chatted with her as she sipped clear liquor through a thin plastic cocktail straw. She was joined by a tall, dark-haired guitar player, about my age, in a black shirt with tasseled sleeves that went with the tassels on Molly's white jacket and miniskirt. She spoke into his ear. He nodded somberly, and gave Molly's ass a possessive squeeze. Molly tossed him a stage smile and twirled away.

She walked to my table. I could see she was scared, which bolstered my confidence. Her eyes were heavily made up for the show and they looked bruised in the darkness of the bar. Fifty feet away, people drank and watched television. Molly looked over at the guitar player, shook her head *no*.

I said, "Is he your bodyguard?"

"His name's Adam. He's sweet," Molly said. "He's kind of protective, that's all." Her voice was higher in conversation than in song, and it was ragged from the night's work. Molly said, "At least he's not after money."

"I'm not after money. You said so yourself the other day, remember?"

Ever-so-slightly, Molly trembled. She said, "I heard... I read about you in the paper. You kidnapped that senator, then let him go, and he won't press any charges. I don't get it. If he told *you*, why didn't he tell the cops?"

I said, "Relax." I told Molly about kidnapping Watkins, how he was on the sauce again, and that I'd forced him to talk. I described his guilt and his pain.

Molly crinkled her eyes. "Aw, shit. He didn't act no worse than lots of old geezers. Hell, I waved him down."

"So you're not bothered he wrecked his career because he had you in the car when it happened?"

"He was *drunk*, Sherlock. That's how he wrecked his precious career."

Suddenly her eyes were wet, and wiping them Molly smeared dark makeup down her cheeks. She took a length of hair and draped it down her left arm. She stroked it. Molly said, "You got like five minutes. Adam thinks you're Joe's cousin and we got to hash out a business thing."

I looked through the shadows, to the bar. Adam sat next to the band's drummer. He shot me a hostile sneer.

I said, "I need to know why you didn't call Sheriff Niles, and tell him what happened. I can understand you panicking at first, but I mean later. See, if you won't tell me why you didn't contact the police, I might have to do it myself."

129

She grabbed some streaming hair and roughly looped her hand around it like it was red rope. Molly said, "Why didn't *you* tell Cliff?"

"Because I promised the senator I wouldn't."

Molly smiled, a genuine bloom. "That's total bullshit."

I said, "It's not bullshit. Look, since I'm sure your husband was murdered, I don't see any reason to ruin Watkins' life anymore than it already is. If it comes out he was touching your legs just before it happened, it could kill him."

Molly tugged hard on her coiled hair, twisting her head down and to the side. "At first," she said, "I didn't call the cops because I was so scared. And once I wasn't, I didn't want to get involved."

"Why did you run up the hill after Joe got hit?"

"The other way's the ocean. Duh. I was running away."

"But what made you scream? Senator Watkins says you screamed like hell once you got up the hill."

Her eyes went flat, squinting. They were like a lizard's eyes peering from under a rock. Her sudden stillness told me I'd rung the right bell.

"What did Joe say on the phone? I know he called you. What made you rush up to Sunset, middle of the night?"

Molly said, "I don't really have to talk to you at all."

I said, "Where was your Bronco? Why were you hitchhiking? Can't you see I'm trying to keep you out of trouble? If I can find the responsible party, you can get on with your life."

She dropped the hair. Her round face wore a look of frazzled defeat; Molly may have been in her middle twenties, but she was high miles.

Molly whispered, "Go away. Just go away."

I leaned forward, trying to make her eyes meet mine. "I'm going to hound you until you tell me why you were hitchhiking. Until I get answers, wherever you go, I won't be far behind." I stood without knowing it. My words rained upon her brassy hair, "Why were you hitchhiking up the coast at two o'clock in the morning?"

She grabbed gobs of her hair and flipped them back. I sat down. Her move.

Molly said, "I got a fuckin' flat tire. Is that good enough for you?"

"Maybe, but what did Joe say on the phone that brought you up there in the middle of the night?"

The small corner table shook under her jitters. She looked out past outdoor walkway lights to the black bay. A tear made a wet, shiny line down her left cheek. Molly wiped it away. I sneaked a look at the bar and there was Adam straining to see us in the meager light. I prayed to God he wasn't a gold digger. And while I was at it, I put in a request that Molly Wells didn't have anything to do with the death of her husband.

I said, "Does Mr. Protective over there know about you going up to Sunset that night?"

Molly shook her head. Her eyes dripped glossy tears.

I said, "Okay, let's get it over with. Tell me what Joe said on the phone. You do understand, don't you? I'm going to bird dog you until you help me find out who killed him."

Molly smeared makeup around her face. She looked at me; she looked out to the bay again.

I said, "If it gets out you were there, Kate will use it to try to cut you out of community property. You'll become a suspect."

Molly seemed to search my face for something she could count on, something she could trust, much the same as she had that afternoon in her trailer when she had hidden so much from me.

I said, "Other than the police, I'm the only game in town. You choose."

"Okay, you bastard. Joe told me if I'd meet him at the ranch, he'd let me in on the deal of a lifetime. He said it was all set."

"What was it this time? Stolen TVs? A snow-making machine, so people can ski from Garston Ridge down to the ocean?"

"He wouldn't tell me. He said I had to meet him at the ranch to find out. I went because he sounded like he finally hit the jackpot. I

131

could tell by how he talked. Is that good enough for you, you son-of-a-bitch? Yeah, I knew he wanted to get back together. Yeah, I took advantage of it."

Adam began walking toward us.

Molly said, "Will this shut you up? When I got to the road up there, car lights were coming at me. I started screaming. All I know is, I fell down as the car went by. I don't know if the driver saw me or heard me. The car was *flying*. I got up and ran south. I had to cross the creek by the campground. I took trails down to where I got the flat tire. I couldn't get cell reception to call a tow—I know a guy. I was scared to death somebody was going to see me. You don't have a clue about what it's been like. But now you're going to know. I drove on the flat for…"

Adam arrived, and cut her off. "You're done talkin'." He rolled his shoulders like an old-time movie cowboy. Maybe John Wayne seen on a DVD with Mommy and Daddy. He said, "We're out of here."

Adam pulled Molly to her feet. Then he had her moving. The heels of her white cowboy boots clonked across the floor.

She didn't protest, so neither did I. They passed in front of the now-empty stage. Molly's head rested on his arm—abruptly she tore herself away. She came toward me, her body low, her boots skimming the floor.

I stood. "Molly?"

Adam took a couple of steps after her, stopped and looked around at those watching.

Moving quickly toward me, Molly said, "The reason I never said was…"

Her wild hair blocked view of her face. She was barely able to keep her balance as she advanced.

I put my hands out. "Molly?"

She said, "I'm *so scared*."

Adam ambled up behind Molly, and put his arms around her skinny shoulders in a kind of lover's lasso.

I stepped toward her. "What's wrong? Tell me."

Molly's ragged voice wafted through wads of red hair. "It was a cop car. A *cop* car."

"What?" I didn't know if I heard her correctly.

She nodded, a kind of confirmation message, as Adam turned Molly and guided her away. They passed through a back door to outside. Stunned, I sat for a minute. *Cop car cop car cop car. Cop car cop car.* It was like waking up with a dumb pop song stuck in your head.

I got up and headed out of The Tides. Somebody lobbed a drink at me. It shattered against the lobby wall. I ignored the crash, ignored the profanities that came with the thrown glass, and stepped into the cool night. All I could think about was Molly saying *cop car.*

I figured it had to be Doug Kolatch driving, because he was the arresting officer. Kolatch was dead. Joe Garston was dead. Watkins was guilty mostly of being a fool. Molly was... I didn't know what Molly was except none too bright and in a tough spot.

I drove north. At that late hour few sets of headlights crossed mine. Eventually, I reached Sunset. About a mile out of town I passed where Joe was hit. At Garston Ranch road I turned right and went uphill. I wasn't sure what I was going to tell Kate about my conversation with Molly. I felt pulled in several directions at once. Each of those directions was driven by partial identification with the woes of people. Allan Watkins. Kate Garston. B-B Stiving. Cliff Niles. Anne Simpson. Molly Wells or Molly Wells Garston. Me.

What did we have in common? We're all part of the same struggle. We're human, and though we share more than ninety-eight percent of our DNA with chimpanzees, we are a million times more complex. We confuse love with desire, we confuse needs with greed. We at times know we are making the wrong choice but choose to make that wrong choice with conviction. If there are gods above, they are surely laughing at us much of the time.

Sixteen

Stairs creaked under my footsteps. I halted, tried going alongside the wall of the staircase, but the stairs cried just the same. I wanted to slip into bed with Kate while she slept.

From her room I heard, "How did it go?"

I stopped, so I wouldn't have to speak over creaking wood, and to hear the rise and fall of her voice without distraction. I said, "You shouldn't have waited up."

"I didn't. I conked out about eleven, but woke up and couldn't get back to sleep."

I reached the landing, which was big enough to hold a quartet of Shaker chairs set around a battered California mission-style table. As with many places in that house, the table was a depository for business and family records. To the right was a narrow hallway, three bedrooms and a bathroom. Left was Kate's room, which I later learned had been the bedroom of her parents.

The door was open. A bedside lamp was on. Next to the green lamp was the pistol that had been in B-B Stiving's quarters, the barrel of which Kate had pressed her lips on, the gun that had blown a hole in the bunk house ceiling.

I stepped in. Kate threw back the blanket. She was naked; my blood jumped. Her dark hair looked too freshly brushed for one who had been sleeping. A lustrous darkness glowed below her waist.

I pointed to the gun. "What's that for?" I sat on the bed and kicked off my shoes. A minute before, I was tired after managing curve after curve for the last thirty night miles of twisty highway. I wasn't tired anymore.

Kate said, "After you left, it was so silent. I got kind of paranoid. I didn't like knowing there was a loaded gun out there."

She leaned forward and put her arms around me. It felt good. I turned and kissed her. She had gargled away any hint of tobacco. There wasn't another soul within a square mile. I took off my clothes and slipped into the toasty bed. The walls were vertical slats of heart redwood milled a hundred years ago.

Kate said, "Well, how was the little dollop?"

I said, "I don't think Molly's a bad person. She's just not what you'd call bright."

I clicked off the lamp. Our sides touched. Her skin was warm, her hair smelled of coconut shampoo. I put an arm around Kate and kissed the top of her head.

"Whenever I think about Molly," Kate said, "I see a little rag doll with a voice like a toothache."

"Have you ever heard her sing?"

"Amazing, isn't it? It's the one thing she can do. She's like a whole other person when she's out there on stage."

We didn't go on about Molly. Whereas the night before had been a venting of desires, in this darkness we moved slowly, feeling each other everywhere. Soft niches, solid corners, hillocks and valleys. We were explorers. The tips of our fingers traversed new land.

I wanted to tell Kate about a cop car racing by Molly on the dirt road, Kate's dirt road, above where her brother had been killed. I thought—amidst kissing and stroking—I thought of saying Molly had told me about Joe's call, driving to the coast, hitchhiking, fleeing. I could say Molly had confessed to me. That way I could tell Kate about the police car, and she wouldn't know I had previously known about Molly's hitchhiking from Senator Watkins.

She said I felt good in her hands. Down there. I put my right hand inside Kate, down there.

She said, "Your shape with your hand, it's hot. It makes you seem more insistent."

I was still thinking I had to find a way to tell her about Molly, hitchhiking, and the cop car. But I couldn't resist her milking fingers. Or the way she opened her mouth while we kissed. Everything spun till we knew what was next. I drove myself home, then withdrew till just the tip of me was inside her. Kate's teeth flashed in darkness.

I drove home again, harder. And home, home, home until the old mahogany bed creaked like a ship in rough seas.

Kate pulled her mouth away. Her words blew heat into my mouth. "There's something I have to tell you."

"Tell me everything."

She licked the side of my face. We plowed into each other.

Kate said, "I'm…" She gulped, and got out, "I'm slowly going broke."

She lost her breath. I was almost over the mountain. Kate lifted her hips and gave me a straight shot through her. Hands wrapped tight around her back, I pulled Kate into me so hard our ribs strained. Our flesh molded like hot wax.

I said, "Tell me everything about you."

With each thrust the headboard banged against the wall. I heard wood splinter.

Kate wheezed, "I like tongue, too."

Sunday morning at the Garston ranch. We wandered around downstairs, not quite sure of how to be with each other. I thought about the many ways places inhabit people as much as people inhabit any place. Kate was proof of that. This led to thinking the reason many of us feel incomplete inside may be that we don't stay put long enough to let our surroundings soak into us. To inhabit us. The strength of a tree depends on the health of its core. From there comes the most beautiful wood. Maybe the curse of California isn't only that it changes quickly, endlessly, but that by moving from place to place so often we never allow any one place to make us whole.

We ate breakfast at the redwood slab table, eggs and bacon and coffee that smelled as good as if we were camping. Soft blue light flooded the kitchen.

Kate wore a beige T-shirt, white panties, nothing else. She said, "How come you haven't asked me about going broke?"

"It's none of my business."

Kate said, "You haven't let that stop you before."

"I guess my mind's been on other things, you know?"

Her brows drew together in a look of seriousness that bordered on strain. Kate said, "I can't decide how I feel about you being twenty-five." Her eyes crinkled, and around them spread crow's feet. "How do you feel about me being thirty-eight?"

My face went hot, and right then it was established that I was more uncomfortable with the difference in our ages than Kate. I said, "It's probably better to just let things happen." I scooped up plates and brought them to the sink. I turned on a faucet that was older than me. I spoke over spraying water. "Is there a usual plan around here for Sundays?"

"No. But my quarterlies have to be in the mail in three days, and they're not done yet."

I asked what she meant.

"Quarterly taxes. We used to have an accountant do 'em. Now it's just me and the good ole I.R.S."

I returned to the long slab table. Kate looked at me in a focused, direct way.

She said, "I've never talked to anyone about how..." She tried again. "People think I'm this rich bitch who owns all this land, when actually I'm struggling just like everybody else. I work like hell seven days a week and half the time we still go backwards."

I said, "Day before yesterday, you said you'd just made a bundle.

On some framing contract for a mall in Redding."

Kate sighed, this time in a way that had nothing to do with pleasure. "It's a reprieve. The profit will equal three months' bills. Including for a mortgage on this house, the first one it's ever had." She ran both hands back through dark hair. "Come on," Kate said, standing, reaching for me, "the stuff on this table depresses me."

We went to the parlor. She opened the drapes. Descending yellow hills, dark treetops, and the faraway lighthouse appeared through the square windows like hand-tinted snapshots of days gone by. Wandering, Kate gestured to the old landscape paintings, a flintlock rifle above the fireplace, a hundred objects in the Sunset County museum that was her living room.

She said, "I'll sell every goddamn timber parcel if I have to, but nobody gets this house. I'll burn this place down before I'd sell it."

Kate stared up at the wagon-wheel chandelier. She looked lost. Her chin dropped and she held it in both palms. She cackled half a dozen notes of an indecipherable song, snapped her head. Kate was laughing as she came to me on the couch, but she was on the verge of tears.

Kate whispered, "I'm a little teapot."

She worked her arms around my middle. I stroked the top of her rocking head. There was no way to respond to the odd declaration.

"Why are you losing so much money?"

Kate sat up, turned toward the windows and beheld gauzy squares of her private, lonely paradise. "It's a long story."

I said, "I'm not exactly busy this year." I rubbed her hip, over panties, with an open hand.

Kate said, "For one thing, the corpos clear-cut too much virgin forest in the boom of the early 2000s. Then the amount of old growth product dropped like hell, and that makes it damn near impossible to get permits to cut choice wood today. Which is where an independent like us can turn big profits. Then there's the problem of giving companies foreign tax credits for un-milled lumber they export. I say 'they' because I won't do it. It eliminates local jobs. Get this, one out of every four trees cut in the West is shipped overseas."

Kate sat up. She reached for a pack of Camels that she kept on the end table next to the duck teacups. She lit one, drew in smoke, blew it toward the wood ceiling.

I said, "You sound like you want to make American great again."

Kate reached across the couch and gave me a shove. "Go to hell. I'm just telling you what outsiders think. They think it all comes down to cutting trees for money, or saving trees for parks. Hell, we got tracts that to do an EIR would cost way more than we'd clear in an okay market. I can't log 'em, and they're no good for parks because they're thirty-forty miles from any decent roads."

Kate took a puff, snuffed out her cigarette in an ash-filled duck teacup. She scooted over, rested her head on my shoulder. I pulled her close. I saw Kate in a rather heroic light. She was fighting to retain the family legacy, trying to help the local economy, do the right thing.

Kate said, "I hate whiners. I refuse to turn into one."

"You're not whining."

"The only way to explain why I can't make more profit is to complain about corpos, EIRs, taxes and tree-huggers."

Kate got up and started across the room. She must have felt my eyes on her rear and long legs, because just as she passed under the wood archway she broke for the stairs. Her bare feet pounded them.

I chased her upstairs. She slammed her bedroom door, locked it. I banged on the door to no avail. Inside, a dresser drawer opened.

Kate said, "Go away. I can't waste my time trying to educate a youngster like you. I've got work to do."

"Quit bragging."

Another drawer slid open, then shut. I heard her getting dressed on the other side.

She said, "You want to come to the mill with me?"

I was leaning against the solid dark door. "No, I'm going to town."

"Oh? Annie Simpson catch your fancy? I hear you two were dancing pretty fancy at Art's last week."

"Maybe we were," I teased, "but my date's with the grocery store. We're down to tin cans around here. And I want to talk with Niles. See if I can get him to talk about the case."

In my head I saw Kate's room littered with our clothes. I was expecting her to open the door at any second. I heard the squeak of springs, Kate sitting on the bed. Then what I took to be the sound of her pulling on jeans.

I said, "If you'll just let me get my pants, I'll be on my way. You want me to pick up anything in town?"

The springs creaked. Kate came to the door and toyed with the knob.

I said, "Cut it out. Let me in."

Yet again, the bed springs creaked. A rustling, sliding sound told me Kate had slipped off her jeans.

She said, "I unlocked the door. It's chow time. Come and get it."

Seventeen

Before I went to Sunset General for groceries, I drove through town and pulled into the lot at the county government complex. A young male deputy was behind the counter. I asked to speak with Niles. The deputy invited me to take a seat. I heard him talk low into the dispatch radio. A minute later, the deputy gave me directions to where I could meet the sheriff.

I drove south. It occurred to me that—urban and rural—in the West we spend more time alone in our cars than alone with our lovers. Added to the thought was that most people spend more time looking at a computer screen than at other people. No wonder so many of us are depressed.

I turned right onto a one-lane road that followed a westerly bulge in the coastline. A few houses were tucked beneath redwoods. I smelled the ocean but couldn't see it. The road became gravel, and after a quarter mile the gravel ended. I parked. I walked down a swathe of dirt and then sand that dropped precipitously to a stream.

Sheriff Niles was fly-fishing, in uniform, just up from where the gurgling stream met ocean waves; there was a broad foamy shoal at the mouth of the stream. He had driven down the rutted dirt road and parked his blue-and-white patrol car above the tide line. Its trunk was left open. Partially sunk in shallow water, Niles wore green rubber fishing waders over patrolman's slacks, and a safari hat with fishing flies hooked all over it. Tucked into the top left pocket of his shirt was a walkie-talkie.

I called his name. He couldn't hear me over the waves. A gust came off the sea, spreading glittery ripples upstream. Niles whipped blue line quickly, like he was lashing a horse. He cast a dark fly onto the gray-green water.

Niles saw me, waved. He was playing in the line. I walked along the edge of the stream. The sandy bank gave and I barely avoided slipping into the water.

I said, "No church today?"

Niles pointed to the Pacific, back to a clump of redwoods at the bend upstream, and to a cloud swirling above. He said, "If this isn't God's house, where on earth is?"

"You and I think a lot alike."

He grunted doubt and trudged out of the stream. The labor of making it to land left Niles short of breath. He set the rod and reel across the car's top. He held onto a fender and began working off the heavy rubber hip waders.

"Had lunch?" he asked.

"As a matter of fact, no."

Niles got the waders off and flopped them onto the hood of the police car. He lifted his hat, wiped sweat off his head and replaced the hat. I'd never seen him like this: quiet. Pensive. Niles went to the open trunk and drank from a clear plastic gallon jug of water. He plucked out two pies. In both he stuck a fork.

He said, "Almonds are mentioned seventy-three times in the Old Testament alone."

"I'll take your word for it."

Sheriff Niles handed me a lemon tart with four almonds placed on top like arrows on a compass. His pie was pink, and he was already eating as his rotund frame met the sandy ground near me. He said, "Nobody makes a rhubarb pie like my wife."

The stream gurgled. Wind combed the tops of redwoods.

I said, "I went and saw Molly Wells last night. I have to talk to you about it."

Nodding, chewing, Niles said, "You sat in back. You passed her some kind of message. You drank two beers. After the show you went off in the corner with her. No?"

"I did. She told me some things you should know."

Niles laughed, shook his beefy jowls and looked up. "What should I know, Mr. Jeffrey Taylor? Huh? I'll tell you something you don't know. The Garston case is closed. Watkins plea-bargained it. I got the call this morning."

"That's not possible. Senator Watkins is going to fight this to the end. He's got to. It's his *life*." I tried to calm myself, to lower my voice. "What kind of plea bargain are you talking about?"

"D.U.I., involuntary manslaughter, the whole nine yards. He gets a suspended sentence and a ten-thousand dollar fine. Can't drive for twenty-four months. And a hundred hours of community service." Niles shoveled a wedge of pie into his mouth. He said, "I don't like it, but it's reasonable. Joe's blood alcohol was one-point-four percent. That means he couldn't see straight. Hell, he probably couldn't see crooked. It makes it harder to refute Watkins' saying Joe was bent over in the middle of the road. If he'd forced a trial, he might well have walked."

"Did you get sold out by the D.A.? What's his name, Chapman?"

Niles shook his jowls again. They flapped sideways like fans. "I don't blame Roger. He got calls from three members of the County Board of Supervisors reminding him it would strain the budget to hold a trial. Watkins could've strung the case out. Whether I like it or not, there's a certain way of doing things when you deal with a politician of that stature."

Niles scooped in pie. "I been told to inform Kate about the arrangement."

I caught myself eating quickly, part of my old habit of trying to please other people. I said, "Whoever put Joe in the middle of the highway is a different question. I don't see it as having much to do with the senator. So I'm kind of glad he has the sense to throw in the towel."

"You glad enough about it to tell Kate for me? When I talked to her on the phone the other day, I got the impression you two are keeping company."

I said, "I won't deny it." Behind me a big wave hit the shoal: *Boom.* I jumped a little. Foamy water hissed.

Niles said, "I'd be awfully thankful if you'd tell her for me. What the hay, you've talked to her and Watkins more than I have. Remember, he gets a five-year suspended sentence, ten-thousand dollar fine, and he can't drive for two years. Plus community service." Niles shoveled in the last chunk of sweet pink pie. "You owe me one, no? For not running you in for basically kidnapping Watkins, and reckless driving. I took heat for not bringing you in."

I said, "I'll tell her. But I got a feeling this plea bargain for Watkins bugs you more than it bugs me."

Niles waved the fork back and forth. "It ain't the plea. We're burying a deputy tomorrow, that's what bugs me. That's what makes me still interested in the case, theoretically closed or not."

"Can I take that to mean you haven't got any leads on where Stiving is, or any breaks in Joe's case?"

Niles said, "You can take it any way you want."

Sunlight bounced off Niles' tin plate. He tossed it and the fork aside. He had a long slug of water from the clear plastic container, and capped it. Sheriff Niles leaned back, elbows in soft, sandy ground.

He said, "What did you want to talk to me about?"

I recounted my conversation with Molly, making it sound like I had finessed her into confessing. I left out the senator's earlier confession about picking her up and getting flirty with her. I said nothing that would put me in a bad light. I told the sheriff about Molly running away uphill and a police car whizzing by her.

Niles had idly sunk into the ground, but mentioning the cop car

144

brought a shot of heat from him. "So Molly was comin' up to meet Joe. Well, oh well. How interesting life can be."

I said, "Well yourself, Sheriff. What about a cop car up on the fire road, where I know damn well Joe Garston came tumbling down from?"

He nodded. "You bear bad news, brother." Niles sat up. In a finicky manner he brushed sand off his heavy forearms. He said, "I don't know what the hell Doug was doing up there, but a minute later he's busting Watkins down on the highway. It's likely Joe had been up there with him, but I don't really know that. I simply don't know nothin' much." Niles brushed away more grains of sand. "I'll tell you what's funny though. This morning I go to Molly's, to inform her of the plea. Legally, she's still Joe's spouse. Anyway, she's not there. So I go to the boyfriend's house in Cloverdale. You remember him from last night?"

"Of course."

"That's when things get funny. This Adam kid tells me Molly went to visit an Aunt Barbara in the Sierra foothills for a few days. To, and I quote, 'chill out.'" Niles caught a breath. "At first I don't have an opinion if it's true, or if it might mean she ran off with somebody else. You never know with Molly-Dew." Under the safari hat his forehead was pink as rhubarb, and dotted with beads of sweat. "Now you come tell me a story about Senator Watkins, Molly, and if she's not out of her gourd, it also implicates Doug K. This case ain't near closed, a Watkins plea deal or not."

Niles geared up for rising out of the sand. He grunted, made it to his feet and while walking away a few steps he unsnapped the top shirt pocket and extracted the walkie-talkie. Niles clicked it and barked: "Wake up down there!"

There was a crackling noise, then, "Yes, sir."

"I got no cell reception here. So get District Attorney Chapman on the phone for me. Tell him I'll be at his place in thirty minutes. If he ain't home, try Judge Hall's. If he ain't there, try his folks down in Oakmont and get back to me pronto. Get back to me no matter what." Niles put the walkie-talkie back in his pocket. He let his hefty frame settle against the side of the blue patrol car.

I watched this, knowing I'd betrayed Kate by telling Sheriff Niles things I'd hidden from her.

Niles lifted his hat, ran a hand over his carpet of hair. "Now let me get this straight. Joe told Molly he was going to make a killing in a week?"

"Or words to that effect."

"Well, Joe was down in Mexico the tenth of August. I know that on account he had to fly because he's lost his license, and he was listed as on a flight out of Oakland. I figured it was just another week of drinking. He'd do that, fly south and get drunk for a week—hey, Taylor, you've stirred up a friggin' hornets' nest."

I said, "Will Watkins' hiding from the police what he did as far as picking up Molly, will it negate his plea?"

"I'm a cop, not a prosecutor. But if I had to guess, he'll get some kind of threat for hiding evidence, but it'll go away. Goodbye."

He folded the hip waders and put them in the trunk of the car. He broke the rod down and did the same with that. I got out of the way while he worked the patrol car around and gunned it up steep dirt and sand and over the hill. I knew Niles was about as excited as he got, or at least as preoccupied as he got, because he forgot his forks and pie tins.

Eighteen

The phone rang as I worked the key Kate had given me into a round, rusted lock on the front door. I came in with grocery bags, to make things look normal to whomever had been following me. I passed the black telephone in the hall. I'd heard it ringing when I had reached the front door. Kate's recorded voice said, "Sorry I'm not here to take your call, but if you'll leave your number, I'll…"

I set the groceries on a counter in the kitchen. From the hall I heard Kate's mother say she had been contacted by a man who claimed Joe had promised him a partnership in subdividing a forty-acre parcel on Iverson Road. She left the man's phone number, said "Love you," and hung up.

I went out the back door and crossed the untended yard. My ears were filled with humming, the kicking in of adrenaline. It was like the zinging that rolls over a field of power lines; its pitch went up and down like that. I thought about returning to the house for a knife but figured it was wiser not to carry a weapon. Only something bad could come of it.

After talking with Niles I'd gone grocery shopping, then headed back to the ranch. I'd made the turn up Garston Ranch Road, cut through cypress and redwood trees, and started up through the old sheep pastures toward the house. On the first curve I had looked behind me, for a view of the ocean, and caught sight of a dark sedan veering into the long shadow of trees. Now I jogged behind the

147

bunk and carriage houses and dropped into a ravine. I followed the gully downhill, trying to keep my steps quiet. When I reached the cypress trees above the highway, I picked my way along a deer trail. At Garston Ranch Road I went right and walked uphill to behind a dusty Toyota Corolla that had dents in the back bumper.

The car was empty. The doors were locked. Inside were fast-food wrappers from hamburgers, tacos, fries, the works. On the back seat was an olive-green army bag, half filled, though with what I could not see. I sat in shade against the right rear wheel, and waited. Five minutes passed. I heard footsteps coming down the road. The adrenaline started its insistent tune. When the steps became close, I popped up like a jack-in-the box.

I said, "Are you looking for me?"

It was Adam, Molly's boyfriend. He threw me his practiced sneer. He wore a T-shirt with *Party Hardy* and a beach scene splashed in bright colors across its front. He wore ragged cutoff jeans and dark running shoes with no socks. His brown hair was messy, and he seemed even skinnier than he had the night before. Adam put his hands out to the sides, as though for balance, bent his knees, gazed left and then right. He looked like he might draw an imaginary six-gun.

I slid around the car and blocked the driver's door. Adam nodded, vaguely, taking things in. His face and arms were pale, like Molly's.

I said, "Are you looking for me or not?"

Adam said, "That's my car."

"Oh, really?"

He said, "This is a public road."

"It's paved, and it's marked, but once you leave Highway One all this belongs to the Garstons. Maybe you've heard the name."

Adam's next pose was to stand with legs wide apart and put both hands on his hips. He looked silly trying out a threatening stance while wearing a mall T-shirt and ragged cutoffs. I figured to help things along a bit by walking up to him with an outstretched hand. "Listen," I said, "your name's Adam, right?"

I guess he didn't want to look scared, so he put out his hand. My hand went out. Adam looked down at it. He froze at seeing its grotesque form; I slapped him so hard he stumbled off the road. I took his right arm, twisted it behind him, and shoved. Adam grunted at hitting earth. I pinned both his arms up behind him and gave them a good stretching.

Adam said, "Son of a *bitch*."

I kept the pressure steady, not enough to injure him, but enough to encourage cooperation. "Be nice. It makes people want to be nice back."

Adam said, "What's your deal, man?"

I pressed a knee into the center of his back. "My deal," I said, "is I want to know why you were following me."

I shoved him forward, face in the dirt and dead grass beside the road. I slipped his wallet from his jeans and walked away from him.

"Fuck you," he said.

"I think I got a right to know who's following me."

Adam picked himself up. He shook his head, loosened his shoulder sockets and flapped his arms. Adam batted dirt and bits of grass from his hair. He did his best look tough again, but seemed to know it was of no use. He sounded more conciliatory than aggressive when saying, "Give me back my wallet, and I won't have you arrested."

"Just tell me why you were following me." The wallet was of a fake silvery snakeskin. I opened it and found his driver's license: Adam R. Reisfeld. The address was in Cloverdale. He had eleven dollars, a ten and a one, a few Wellbeats business cards, a receipt from a tool rental yard, an ATM card, a Chevron card and a few folded Far Side cartoons. I said, "After you tell me why you're following me, tell me where Molly's Aunt Barbara lives. We can wing it from there."

Adam cursed me again, demanded I give him his wallet and let him into his car, or he was going to walk down to Sunset and file an assault complaint.

I said, "I have a better idea. If you'll take me to Molly, I'll give you a thousand dollars. I mean it. Here." I produced my own wallet. I counted out eight musty fifty-dollar bills, fanned them at Adam like tickets, and transferred them into the billfold of his wallet.

"Here's a down payment. See, we can be buddies."

His dark eyes widened, then narrowed, watching me tuck away the money. He said, "You're one weird son-of-a-bitch."

"That's right. And there are six hundred more weird dollars in the trunk of my car that are yours if you take me to Molly."

Adam shook his head again, looked at his hands. "Give me my wallet or I'm going to the cops."

"Sounds good," I said, and began walking up the road.

"Hey!"

I walked briskly.

"Hey, wait a minute!"

I didn't look back. I heard footsteps on asphalt.

He caught up with me. Adam said, "Hey, I came out here looking for Moll and saw you driving up the highway."

I stopped walking. I said, "*Hey*, why did you follow me?"

"Last night, she said you were Joe's Cousin. But you didn't act like no cousin. You sat too close to her. So when I seen you driving up One, I followed you. For all I know Moll's up at the ranch, clearing out her old things. Maybe you're helping her."

"Adam, my name is Jeff Taylor. I'm working for Joe's older sister, Kate. I'm trying to find out if somebody threw her brother in front of Senator Watkins' car. I should say who threw him in front of the car. I know it wasn't Molly, but that's about it."

Looking down the road, into the tunnel of trees lining it, I saw a little chunk of green sea. It rose, and a white wave curled forward. Then it was green again. I could look at stuff like that all day. I knew I'd return Adam's wallet, but I was going to get as much out of him as I could before doing so.

Adam's jaw set as hard as it was able to. "She wakes up this morning. It's like hardly light out, and Moll tells me she's going to visit her aunt for a couple days. That's bullshit and I know it."

"You're probably right," I said.

It was odd, standing next to a guy I'd just popped. But it had gotten him talking. I was worried Kate might come along, on her way home from the mill, and Adam would freeze up.

I said, "If you love Molly, you'll help me find her. Look, somebody killed Joe Garston. Take my word for it. Two days ago, somebody, maybe a guy named Stiving who worked for the Garstons, killed the cop that arrested the Senator." I weighed saying Molly was in the car with Watkins when he had hit Joe, but saw no advantage in opening that worm can. "Now Molly's split on you. See what I'm saying? She could be going somewhere she shouldn't, and she could get hurt."

Adam said, "I'm tired of worrying about poor little Moll Wells Garston. That head case cost us like five gigs. I'll find somebody else to look hot and sing like she's about to die."

Adam folded his arms across his chest. We both looked down the tunnel of trees lining the pavement.

He said, "She ain't worth the trouble she brings. Give me my wallet back and leave the money in." Adam was fidgety. He scuffed his tennis shoes across asphalt, looking everywhere but at me. He massaged his forehead as though it helped him think. "Okay. Let's go back to my car. I'll give you a ride up to the house. That's where the money is, right? You're going to need those other six hundred bucks."

I started walking downhill. I took out his wallet, extracted the fifty-dollar bills and gave it to him. "I'll take a ride. But you're not getting squat unless you lead me to Molly."

The sneer mixed with a snotty grin. "You'll want to buy this. No doubt."

We reached the purple Corolla. Adam unlocked the door and got in. He reached over and unlocked the door for me. I swept McDonald's wrappers off the seat. When I sat, my feet were buried in paper trash.

Adam started the Toyota and headed up the hill. He said, "I never thought I'd do something like this."

I said, "Fall in love with somebody who drives you crazy? It happens all the time."

The road paralleled a low mossy fence of rotting wood slats.

"No," Adam said. "I never thought I'd sell somebody out."

Nineteen

I called Kate at the mill.

She said, "What took you so long?"

"Is anybody around who can hear you?"

"What's wrong?"

"Nothing, necessarily. It's a semi-long story. I don't know where to start. Let me just ask you if someplace called The Gaines Tract means anything to you."

She said, "That's up on the Lost Coast. My dad picked it up for back taxes about twenty years ago. Goddamn it, tell me what's wrong."

"I don't know." In my head I saw Kate as I had left her, in jeans, a white tank top. I saw her brush back dark hair. I said, "I think Molly may have gone up to this Gaines Tract. I don't know why, but I'd guess it's not for a nature seminar. But let me tell you other stuff first."

I told Kate about going to the sheriff's office to look through my notebook and sniff for information. I told her about going to where Niles was fishing where a stream reached the ocean, about the plea bargain, how Niles had gone to tell Molly about it, and she had disappeared.

Kate said, "She doesn't have any Aunt Barbara. Not that I ever heard of."

I said, "That figures. But then, listen, on my way up the ranch road

I see someone's following me. I go inside and sneak down through the trees and come up behind him. It turns out it's Molly's boy toy. His name's Adam Reisfeld. You know him?"

"Of course not."

"Well, I pushed him around a little and made him talk. Actually, I paid him a thousand bucks, too."

Kate said, "Why the hell would you do that?"

"I'm having fun giving away your money and the senator's money. It's like Monopoly money. Besides, a deal's a deal. I got Adam to give me a lead to Molly, but it turned out to be more. He gave me a map he says he drew from one Molly got in the mail yesterday. He says she hid it from him, so… Right now it doesn't matter how he got it. You better come home."

Kate was home in thirty minutes. We went into the kitchen and she lit a cigarette. The moment of truth, so to speak, arrived.

The honorable thing would have been to level with her. Tell Kate I'd hidden the senator's confession about Molly from her to protect him, because he was basically innocent and because I had given Watkins my word. The honorable thing would have been to tell Kate I'd hidden what Molly told me at The Tides because everything I learned from Molly had stemmed from Watkins' earlier confession about picking her up. I should have told Kate I'd been afraid that if I admitted hiding things from her in the first instance, I might never see her again. I should have put my cards on the table. Now that I'd told Cliff Niles about Molly's hitchhiking, sooner or later everything would come to light.

I wasn't up to such a moment of truth, so I handed Kate the map I paid Adam Reisfeld a thousand dollars for. I turned on the overhead light in the kitchen as Kate looked at the hand-drawn map.

I said, "She gets her mail at a P.O. box in Ukiah. They went there yesterday." Outside, afternoon wind fluttered across the old windows of the house, sounding like bird wings. I said, "Adam says when Molly went through her mail, she opened an envelope and got all nervous. He decided to pretend he didn't notice. Later, he found it under a dresser, at his place, when she went to the cleaners to pick up her clothes for the show. He copied the map quick as he could. She comes back from the cleaners and announces she has to go visit this fictitious Aunt Barbara to get away from all the turmoil. Then she splits, just saying she'll be gone for a few days."

The map was in black ink on the white backside of a flyer announcing appearances by the Wellbeats at George's Saloon in San Rafael. Adam had copied from what he described as a photocopy of a county parcel map. Written in were longitude, latitude, the distance from Highway 101 and the distances from the ocean. Across the top: "Gaines Tract." A line wiggled through the map, with "Sulphur Creek" written next to it. Below the creek, on a spot near the right-hand edge of the map, was a large X with "Hidden Valley" printed next to that. In the top right corner was, "Sept. 10, 11-12:30."

Kate said, "Was there was a return address on the envelope?"

"Nothing on the envelope but her P.O. box number and the zip code."

"Do you think he knows who sent it?"

"No. To Adam it's just another crazy Molly situation. Right now he's going to Cloverdale to pack up her stuff that's at his place. He says he'll dump it outside her trailer. He's done with her."

Kate walked around the long slab table. Her face had the batty look that sometimes came over it. She said, "Joe knew the Gaines property. He said he was going to bottle the sulphur water from the creek and sell it. He was up there a lot a few years ago, showing people around, trying to get them to invest. Sometimes Molly went with him. It was another of their sure-fire million-dollar ideas."

"Who would Joe meet out there? If he still could."

Kate ground out her cigarette on a white dinner plate. I stood and hugged her before she could walk away. I was nervous, scared and wired, and feeling guilty. I held her tight and rocked her side to side.

Kate and I had begun building something and I didn't want to lose it. Or, deep down, did I want to wreck it? I still don't know for sure.

She said, "I'm not going to be able to stay here. It'll drive me crazy if we don't go check it out."

The way she held me, I noticed with relief, was as clingy and desperate as the way I held her. I said, "I sure as hell would like to know who sent the map. But I don't know about going a hundred miles into the middle of nowhere."

Kate said, "There's a cabin on the property. Well, it's more like a shack. We can hike in tonight, and tomorrow we can check this out. Why not? Call it good luck with the timing."

Assuming she wouldn't, I said, "Do you think we should tell the police?"

Kate didn't answer, which was her answer. She went upstairs to pack. Half an hour later we were heading north with me at the wheel of her pickup. I buzzed with a glee that was associated with getting away with my lies, and the nervy elation that comes with tiptoeing around the law.

For two hours we followed the coast. At about five o'clock, as the coastline veered westward, the highway turned inland into thick virgin forest. A few miles later we left it for a series of dirt roads where we didn't see any buildings or another vehicle. The roads all seemed connected, as in a maze, and were the same, one lane of dirt, no signs or landmarks. Kate simply said go left or right or go straight. We spoke little.

Kate had me pull off the road and poke my way through woods so thick I turned on the headlights. We bounced around trees and dark brush as if navigating a minefield, and eventually hid the truck behind a cluster of redwoods. We unpacked gear and provisions. Above us, all around us, rigid conifers blocked the day's remaining sunlight. Nothing moved. The only sound was the soft falling of our steps on duff. It was as though the world had been divided into outside the virgin forest, and within. It was as if we walked inside a womb.

The trail became steep. We climbed half a mile, topped a ridge. Up there wind blew steady and cool. We drank mineral water, ate red apples and Jack cheese.

Kate smoked a cigarette, ground it out in her palm, and stuck the butt in a front pocket of her jeans. We headed downhill. It was difficult to see a trail. I held Kate's hand and shook off feeling like a kid hiking with my mom in the lonely, early days of our life in Grantsville.

The brisk climbing burned off some of her nervous energy. The earlier anxiousness faded. The expedition began to feel like a lark, a kind of manic foray that for me was a way to placate Kate. It was also buying me time to maneuver around having held out on her. I should really say it was buying me time to figure out how I'd cover up for having lied to the woman who a few days before had become my lover.

Kate said, "I'm going to have to ask sometime. You know, about your hand."

I was relieved by the diversion from worrying over my lies.

"I used to work at the tomato cannery every summer. You get twelve-hour days, six days a week. It was fast money. I'd work the swing shift for extra pay. You harvest under lights from dusk on." I'd told people what happened so many times the words came out like Muzak. I'd told the story so many times I almost didn't hear myself saying it anymore.

"With the lights making glare, you don't see well. I was emptying crates delivered from the field into this huge machine that sliced tomatoes. The first step in making tomato sauce. I was daydreaming and my hand strayed under a crate when I set it down. Maybe a hundredth of a second. It got pulled in, onto the slicer rack. It was stupid. I'd done the same thing a thousand times and wasn't paying attention. It's the one thing they tell you every day: pay attention." I waived my bad hand. Kate's eyes followed it. I said, "That's about all there is to it."

Kate stopped walking. She took my normal left hand with her

normal right hand. "That's not all there is to it. You just described a nightmare that changed your life."

We topped another ridge. Above, through limbs, the gray was turning purple. Kate led without compass or map. We were puffing. I had a drink of water and passed the canteen to Kate.

I told Kate I'd decided that to become a pediatrician would never work. I'd frighten the patients, seem a freak to them. They'd never be able to relax with me. I'd spent my undergrad years dreaming of going to medical school, and suddenly I was lost. I drifted, staying away from other people most of the time, and found myself drinking hard, and alone.

"Out of the blue, Clint Sherman invites me to lunch. Clint's the old guy I told you about. He knows everybody. He played basketball at Sac State back in the day. He'd heard about what happened through an old teammate of mine, and said he could give me work until I decided what to do next. I started out escorting women staffers to parties and being a bouncer. After a while he put me onto more complicated matters."

Kate said, "You sound like quite the young bachelor. I bet you took some of the women you escorted home, too." Before I could protest, Kate said, "By the way, we're here."

A small cabin/shack materialized in the gloam ahead of us. About seven feet high, the little cabin had blended into nightfall. Its walls were stacked logs. It was roofed with logs, peeled chunks of redwood bark, and needles and twigs that fell on it over the years.

We sat. A cooling coat of evening fog sank through the trees. Fresh blisters burned on both of my heels. The hard walking was done, the day was ending. Everything seemed to stop. It was a little like getting out of the car after a long day of driving. I closed my eyes against the quiet and stillness of the womb-like woods.

B-B Stiving stepped out from behind a tree trunk. He said, "I only want what's mine. That's all I expect."

We leaped to our feet as though seared by fire.

Kate yelled: "God!"

I felt so light it was as if I could swim through the murky air.

B-B Stiving did indeed look like a bear, a bear with a machete in its paws. His eyes were dark, barely visible, his head a bush of tangled brown hair. The machete caught speckles of dusky light. B-B rested it on his chest, its tip pointed forward.

Kate said, "Bob, you scared the *hell* out of me."

My heart beat so hard it hurt to breathe.

Kate said, "I was hoping you'd be here." I was amazed at how clear and confident her voice was. "I'm glad to know you're safe."

Stiving smacked himself on the left ear as though trying to knock water from it. He said, "I'm having trouble with it. I mean Doug, not Joe."

Somewhere in the blackish trees, a blue jay squawked.

Kate slipped a navy-blue pack off her shoulders, sat, and glancing at me made it clear I should do the same.

Stiving said, "Did Ed call you?"

Kate said, "What's Ed got to do with this? I don't get it."

Stiving cocked his head to a side. His sweatshirt and jeans were dirt-streaked. Beyond him, tree trunks softly glowed. Carefully, as if afraid to disturb the forest, Stiving sat.

Kate stepped forward and set the canteen in front of him. "I know you've been through hell. God knows how painful it's been. I just wish you'd come to me. To talk."

For a full minute, nobody said anything. Two jays called back and forth on either side of us. I struggled to see. B-B cracked himself on the left ear again.

Kate said, "Put the knife away... Okay?"

He set it down, and looked back and forth, following the bird calls. He took up the canteen Kate had given him and gulped down every last drop of water.

Kate wiped her face. She spoke, her pitch higher than normal, as you would talk to a child. "It shouldn't have turned out like this, you know? Tell me about it."

Stiving's face dropped to between his knees. He shook his head *no, no*. Cool wind licked the trees with a rising whistle. Stiving tilted his huge head toward me. "Why is he here?"

"Jeff's helping me now. We're together on this."

B-B cocked his dirty face to a side again. Clearly exhausted, he popped an open hand against his upturned left ear. He motioned one paw toward me. "I'm sorry about the other night. After you left, Katy was crying. I was trying to cut things off then and there. Keep people from snoopin' around." He rubbed the stubble on his face. "I'm sorry, about everything."

I said, "We're on the same side now. Forget about it."

B-B said, "I'm still *sorry*, man," and slapped his ear again. It sounded like a punch. "Who found Doug?"

Kate said, "Cynthia, when she came home from work."

B-B dropped his head so far between his knees he almost kissed the ground.

Kate said, "I hear she's a mess."

I threw Kate a look, questioning her method. I didn't think it wise to push Stiving. Kate shrugged, went to him and put her hand on his broad back. It reminded me of someone petting a horse.

Kate said, "We're going to get through this."

She began to say something else, but apparently her well of easy words ran dry. The silence that followed seemed to hover at the edges of what we could see in those dark woods, a silence that if left to grow could drive Stiving over the edge. I kept track of the machete.

Kate said, "Bob, whatever happened with Joe, it's not your fault. You were home. It's not your fault."

Stiving's eyes, unblinking, small under his dark bushy hair, looked like fish eyes. Arms anchoring him like poles, he swayed forward, and back, forward and back. Kate patted him on a shoulder again. Stiving pitched forward, stumbled, and caught himself against the trunk of a redwood. He swung his head wildly. "Goddamn it!" Stiving rolled his head, stretching his neck. "I'm glad it wasn't me, Kate. That's the problem. I'm *thankful* it wasn't me. Don't you see how bad that is?"

B-B craned his head, looking up to the black branches, maybe to heaven.

Kate walked, slowly, toward him. "There's nothing you can do. There's nothing anybody can do now but go through with the deal. I assume that's what we're here for."

They were blotchy figures. The bear-like shape stepped forward and banged his forehead against the tree trunk. "Goddamn you Doug! Leave me alone!"

B-B clubbed himself twice on the crown of his head. He reared his head back. Kate went after him. I ran after her and the two of us wrestled B-B to the ground after he banged his head against the tree again. He rolled us across the forest floor, crying out to the ghost of Doug Kolatch that all he wanted was to be left alone. He bucked and kicked like a bull and threw us off in two quick moves, Kate to one side, me the other. From the ground I saw B-B lumber off into darkness. The door to the tiny cabin slammed shut.

"Stay out! I don't want to hurt anybody."

Twenty

Sweating in darkness, mouth bleeding, my face stung from another Stiving boot kick. I was sprawled on redwood duff miles from anyplace I had ever been. I shook sparks from my head, and asked Kate if she were all right. She crossed the bed of twigs and dead needles, and found me. We breathed as hard as after making love. She hugged me with the same desperation as before we left the ranch. All during that afternoon she had swung back and forth between aloof introspection and an almost frantic holding on.

I whispered, "I say work on B-B with regards to what he knows about Joe. After that, leave him to his own fate. We could walk all night and be at that stream tomorrow morning. We've got flashlights. I got a gallon of water in my pack. I don't want to get hung up with this guy because he's an old friend of you and your brother's."

The words came rapidly. The way you talk when you're scared. Kate ran a hand back through my hair. She kissed me on the forehead. I sensed she was trying to calm me.

Kate said, "The other night, you talked about how it hurt you to not be doing anything important in life. You said the idea of finding out who killed Joe had gotten you going again. I feel the same way. My life hasn't been worth much these last few years. Taking care of this, all of it, Joe, Doug, B-B—it might be the way to save everything I've been working for. I'm not saying it will, just there's a chance."

All I could see of Kate were an outline of her face and frame that were slightly darker than the cool damp air around her.

I said, "You sure you know what you're doing?"

Kate said, "I've always believed if I hate something enough, I can beat it."

Before I could chew that over, she pulled her face away and called out, "We're going to have to talk, Bob. There's no way around it."

Silence. Except for wind that with its moisture brought the scent of a redwood forest.

Kate squeezed my arm. "I'm going to go talk to him."

"Don't push him. It's not worth it."

Kate got up from the ground. She went to the glinting machete, picked it up, took a few steps and pitched it into dense blackness. It disappeared without a sound. I barely saw her pass by me and go toward the low cabin. Then I saw a silhouette of her hunched over, sitting, hands wrapped around her knees.

Kate called through the log wall. "It's just us. We're going to talk about what happened."

From inside the cabin came, "It won't let me alone. I'm *glad* Doug took it. I'm glad it wasn't me."

Kate told B-B she understood.

Then it sounded like Stiving was going to break up the log shack with his fists. He swore and punched, and Kate sat there, telling him over and over that they were going to talk.

Digging through fallen tree needles, I found a boulder I could barely wrap my good hand around. If Stiving came out after Kate I was going to smash him over the head with it. Then I'd go for his balls with my well-trained hook hand, rip them so hard even the legendary Bigfoot would keel over.

Kate said, "I'm coming in now. We're going to talk about it."

I jumped to my feet. "*Don't.*"

Kate said, "He's all right now. Isn't that right, Bob? You're all right now, right?"

163

I stepped toward the black shape, the cabin.

Kate walked with one hand skimming a wall, turned the corner, waved to me, found the crude wood handle and swung the door open.

Stiving's voice sounded like it came from a cave. "I been here two nights. Last night I chased some people away I don't think were really there."

I was fifteen feet from the cabin.

Kate stood in the doorway. Like a nurse tending to a patient, she said, "Everything is okay now. We're going to find a way to help you."

Stiving said, "Shut the door."

Kate's shadow moved; the wooden door shut. The black square of stubby cabin loomed in front of me.

Holding the rock in my left hand, I heard Stiving's voice rise, though I couldn't make out words. Kate's voice rose. Their voices leveled off into a drone that meshed with the humming in my ears.

With nothing moving in the woods, and feeling chilled by the settling dampness of fog, I thought about how Kate had said Stiving was basically family. I thought about how country people tend to stick together. I'd seen it while growing up. They could be making plans. I thought of how easily I'd lied to Kate and gotten away with it. She could do the same with me. Easy. Plus, Stiving would want her to act on his behalf, not mine.

After about a dozen minutes of not knowing what was being talked about inside the cabin, anxiety hit me in hot rolling waves. I thought: *I'm getting what I deserve.*

I closed my eyes and tried to slow incoming thoughts by counting my breaths. I failed to slow incoming thoughts, opened my eyes, and saw a shadow coming toward me. The approaching shadow wasn't wide enough to be Stiving. I stood, dropped the stone. My heart thumped violently.

Kate spoke before we touched. "B-B's going to Canada. He'll leave at first light. We'll take his share. He'll send me directions about where to send the money. It's a coke drop all right."

I put my arms around her. I thought that if I were affectionate enough, she wouldn't know my developing thoughts. I kissed her. She kissed back but seemed only to be going through the motions. We were slow dancing in a pool of blackness.

I said, "You sure you know what you're doing?"

Kate's chin came to rest atop my shoulder. Her whisper was cool, moist. "A part of Bob wants to kill Ed, so it's best if he's out of here tomorrow. He's bonkers. I'll give you the details later."

I held Kate firmly and walked backwards, taking us away from the cabin, out of potential earshot. "I want the details now. All of them."

Her voice low, Kate said, "You have about five hundred bucks on you, right? We'll give it to Bob. We'll take his share and eventually see to it he gets made whole. He's going to walk out in the morning, because he says it's better if he and Ed don't see each other."

I'd pulled Kate backwards with me until bumping into a tree. I drew her to the ground, and we sat face-to-face. I couldn't see her facial expression.

I said, "It sounds to me like this Lantis guy is in charge."

Kate said, "Not anymore. It was half Joe's deal, and I'm Bob's proxy. That gives me about three quarters."

She told me B-B said Joe had set up the cocaine deal during his August trip south, to Guaymas, on the eastern shore of the Gulf of California. He had done some minor league buying there before. Joe took the money he got from selling his almost-new Jeep, which he couldn't drive anyway, guns he inherited and their father's gold wrist watches, plus B-B Stiving's life's savings, to make a thirty-thousand-dollar, seventy-five percent down payment on a delivery of cocaine. Joe and B-B had decided to put everything they could muster into one shot at prosperity. They were both tired of living under the drooping wings of Garston Timber.

Joe had come home, and failed to get the remainder of the money from company accounts because unknown to him Kate had taken his name off all but the relatively small cash-flow one.

Kate said, "This just shows how out of control he was."

She went on to say that, desperate, Joe and B-B went to Ed Lantis. They knew Ed used to make money by looking the other way while people grew pot on tracts of his land. This income source had dried up the last ten years after cultivating marijuana became legal in most of California, and most growers had chosen to go legit. By offering Ed a hundred percent return—after the cocaine was cut and sold—Lantis went in for the other ten thousand. He wouldn't even have to touch the merchandise. With Joe getting killed, all that changed.

Kate said Joe getting hit was after he'd gone into town, photocopied and mailed a map of the drop site to Mexico. Joe was paranoid about the internet, ever since watching a YouTube video about how the government was following everything online and over cell phones. Ed figured Joe had copies of a map on him when he'd headed back to the ranch, and since none were listed as found on his person by the county, Ed and B-B had paid a visit to Deputy Doug Kolatch. They asked if he had found anything on Joe he had neglected to give to Sheriff Niles. Kolatch told them to get out. He sounded like he was hiding something. He threatened to play cop with them. An argument ensued. Doug finally said he had what they wanted, reached into a drawer—and drew a gun. B-B saw it coming and wrestled him to the floor. The gun went off. It shot Doug in the chest.

Kate said, "Bob just wants to leave the country. Go to Canada and start over."

She was breathless telling me all this, and I had to act more shocked than I was. I already knew, through Molly's recounting of things, that Kolatch, in a police car, had almost certainly been up on the fire break road when Joe came crashing down onto Highway One.

Kate said, "Bob's crazy with guilt. He was looking to buy some land in Washington with the money he'd clear, but now he just wants money to hide out north of the border." Her hands felt their way up to my face; she rubbed the top of my head. "Here," Kate said, "let me get flashlights out of the pack. I better get back with him before he flips out again."

The three of us shared the log shack. Kate propped up a flashlight so its beam hit the low, thatched ceiling. B-B was sullen. He didn't look at either of us. There were thick rings of darkness below his eyes; now that he had settled down, B-B looked to be grieving. Kate made small talk, which was out of character for her. She was obviously trying to keep the ship steady. I didn't sleep an hour without waking. At dawn, B-B ate most of our provisions. He disappeared into the woods without saying goodbye.

We had cold instant coffee—we couldn't leave smoldering ashes— crackers and cheese, and walked downhill. I couldn't see very far. Vertical lines, redwood trunks, blocked the way. They were like sentries on watch. Their needles dripped the thick fog of the night before, and the forbidding quiet seemed to make any conversation an unnatural intrusion. It was the kind of landscape that turns you inward.

I thought about how strange it was to be walking with the scion of one of the oldest continuously operating lumber companies on the West Coast, and rather than examining timber we were looking to the sky for a drop of illegal drugs. In a way that symbolized what California has become. It wasn't a pleasant thought.

At reaching flat ground, we turned—I'd no idea which direction— and soon began climbing. The ground turned rocky and ahead were hills with granite outcroppings. Kate was taking us in over Forest Service land via a route she figured Ed Lantis or Molly would never take, a route where years might pass without a human being stepping foot. After an hour we reached a narrow highlands valley, Hidden Valley from the map I bought from Adam Reisfeld.

Gray clouds blew across the mountains like smoke. The scent of pine wafted over our backs. We found high ground and sat behind a hump of white rock that was roughly the shape and size of an elephant.

I saw Sulphur Creek twisting down the valley's heart, a quarter mile away. The wind made flute-like whistling echoes off the rock. Kate and I kept low, out of sight. Leaning against one another, we talked in a kind of quiet shorthand. Kate put a cigarette between her lips but did not light it. We took turns looking through my binoculars for Ed Lantis and or Molly Wells.

Near noon, we heard, and then looking up we saw a yellow, twin-engine airplane fly barely above the trees, coming from the south. It flew amazingly low and its groans rebounded toward us. I trained my binoculars on the plane.

Kate, an arm looped around my shoulder, said, "Keep your eyes on it. I'll watch for Ed."

The plane dipped even lower. Its wings tipped back and forth. *Hello.* Flashes of yellow reflected sunlight. Engines roared, filling our ears like shouts. The plane was a hundred yards east of us, on a course just high enough to avoid cutting into treetops.

In a low voice, Kate said, "I'm a little teapot."

As if awaiting her incantation, a dark bundle dropped through the gray overcast. Its silent fall took about three seconds. The package disappeared between boulders near the creek.

I sited landmarks. I lifted the binoculars from my eyes, found the landmarks, checked them again with the powerful eyeglasses. I described what I saw to Kate.

She nodded. "Got it."

Kate said, "Here they come, the goddamn vultures. I wonder if either of them even spoke Joe's name on the way in."

Kate pointed. I looked with the binoculars, saw nothing but milky granite boulders and grayish light. Then a man I took to be Ed Lantis, followed by Molly Wells, climbed over a boulder and down between two others, out of sight. They were about two hundred yards from the coke. We were about two hundred yards from the coke. We dumped our packs and headed for the sighted landmarks. I knew that what happened in the next minutes could lend shape to the rest of my life.

It could set me on a path. I headed out so swiftly Kate had to run to catch up.

We clambered over boulders and picked our way toward the stream. We didn't talk. We went around rocks as large as the ex-carriage house Joe Garston had lived in.

From the other side of boulders I heard Molly screech, "Damn Sam. It's over here!"

Lantis called back, "This is like winning fucking lotto."

Kate and I slowed, angling toward their voices. We came around a pile of stones, and there were Molly, in jeans and a tiny pink top, brassy hair fluttering like a sheet in the wind, and Ed Lantis. We were staring at their backs and at a brown leather bundle wrapped in criss-crossings of red nylon rope.

Molly hopped up and down like a teenybopper at her first rock concert. Ed Lantis kneeled, his face showing intense focus. His hair was light brown, pulled back into one of those guy-six-inch ponytails held together by a rubber band. He was a fair amount smaller than me. I took the binoculars off my neck and set them down.

They were only fifty feet in front of us. A hundred feet behind them the Sulphur creek chugged between gray boulders. Lantis took out a knife, a switchblade that erased my original impression that he'd be no problem. He slit the rope webbing and put the knife back in a front pocket of his jeans.

Molly yelled over wind, "Is it okay B-B's not here?"

Lantis said, "Don't worry about B-B. He's got trouble enough already."

Lantis unwrapped three layers of cowhide, which had served as shock absorbers. His movements were deft, like a country doctor called into the emergency room from the range. He wore a green-and-gray checked flannel shirt. He tossed the hides aside and attended to a black duffel bag the peeled hides had revealed. Sitting on his knees, he unzipped it and extracted clear plastic Ziploc baggies, each about the size of a cantaloupe. They contained what looked like powdered sugar.

Lantis opened one. He dried his hands on the thighs of his jeans. He dabbed his right pinky on his tongue and touched it to the cocaine. Lantis withdrew his little finger and sniffed the granules that had stuck to it.

He turned to Molly. I saw half a smile. He said, "It's good shit."

Molly went to her knees and poked a finger into the contraband.

Kate and I edged forward. Molly had a toot. She twitched her nose like a rabbit and turned toward Ed.

Molly said, "Hallelujah!"

We got closer. All around us were big milky boulders. I caught a glimpse of the Sulphur stream. Above, the gray clouds were breaking into shapes like chessmen.

Kate called, "Hello there, partners." She sounded both angry and amused.

They popped off the ground. Molly's face looked like a child's after being caught with a hand in the cookie jar.

Seeing Kate, Lantis recovered quickly. He was, I'd guess, forty years old, with catfish whiskers and a lean face and frame that made him look like he knew his way around outdoor work. His eyes were cloudy. Gold flashed from his teeth. A kind of darkness oozed from his face, like toxic fumes. Lantis said, "Be careful. You're getting into something here you can't handle."

Kate said, "Accept it, Ed. I'm here for Joe and Bob."

Molly's voice finally caught. She looked at me and said, "What are you doing here? I thought you were clean cut."

Splashing sounds came from the stream. We took each other's measure. Ed Lantis was a lean six-footer. His greasy ponytail, his wiry frame and generally coarse look gave him the appearance of a veteran Cossack warrior. And he was in his own territory, light on his feet in black high-top tennis shoes.

I said, "I'm disappointed, Molly. You didn't tell me you were in on this deal." To Lantis, I said, "Molly and I are old friends."

He said, "You must be the college boy I keep hearing about." He added, "With the weird fucking hand."

Those words had about the same effect on me that roaring crowds used to have, while I dribbled the ball up court, the final seconds of a game ticking off the clock and my team was down by one basket: Those words didn't touch me.

Lantis twisted the ends of his catfish mustache as he and Kate continued to check each other out.

Molly looked at me. She said, "When B-B left town—Ed says he didn't really shoot Doug, Doug's gun just went off when they were wrestling. B-B sent me a letter with a map, because it was a deal between Joe, B-B and Ed." She fluffed her hair, wiggled her skinny body. "B-B wrote so I could get Joe's share. He said Joe'd want it that way."

Lantis said, "You know fuckin' B-B. Always looking out for a Garston, even if only by marriage."

Kate said, "Why don't we all sit down?"

We did. A lone hawk sailed above. For one irrational second I thought it could be Joe, checking out the scene. Though I knew it wasn't, I thought: Laugh at us. We're fools.

Ed shook his head. "Listen up. We got a problem. Me and Molly got a legitimate business deal going, and now you show up. Where you shouldn't be. B-B told you, didn't he?"

"No," Kate said. "Joe did." She lied elegantly. "Do you really think my brother would get into something like this without telling me? We may have fought a lot, but we were always still family."

I looked at Kate. I couldn't read her face.

Kate said to Ed, "Before we get into that, I want to know everything you know about my brother's death. I mean every goddamn thing."

This was a kind of accusation that Lantis knew things he wasn't sharing. The two of them locked stares again. The more they stared at each other the more the past seemed to seep into the present.

I said, "We're not leaving until you tell us what you know."

Ed snorted a half-laugh.

Kate said, "Tell me what happened with Joe."

Ed looked up at the fast-moving gray clouds. He blew out a sigh that was louder than the wind. "Katy, we go back too far to let this get out of hand. Go take your... *friend*, be smart and get the hell out of here."

I said, "You can have the dope. But we're not leaving until you tell us what you know about Joe's death."

Lantis said, "Jesus Christ," and stood, which brought us all to our feet. He waved an arm. "I'm going to secure these, and me and Molly are going to walk out of here. In the future, no one is going to talk about this little reunion. It never happened."

He bent over and packed the clear plastic baggies in the duffel bag. Lantis said, "I'm sorry your asshole brother died, but he's gone. It's history, Katy. It is what it is."

Kate said, "Turn around, and put up your hands. Slow-like."

I flinched at the words, and then saw Kate brandishing the pistol that had been in B-B's quarters, and later on her bedside table, the long-handled Colt 45 that had been her grandfather's. I'd no idea she brought it, and hadn't seen it under her thick hooded sweatshirt as we walked to the drop site.

Molly said, "*God*, please don't kill me."

Kate said, "Shut up. Go sit down. Over there." She pointed with the steely barrel of the pistol.

Lantis rose from the duffel bag. His back was to us. His arms went above him, and he waived out of impatience, not fear. His hands flapped like Kate's orders were a tremendous joke. He said, "You won't shoot." His hands stopped flapping, then, no shot fired, he turned around, a look of dark triumph on his Cossack face.

Kate ignored his game. She said, "We bumped into B-B yesterday, at that old Gaines hut. He told me about the two of you going to Doug's. I know you, Ed. I know you enough to know you got B-B

172

fired up about Doug having the map. Get him pissed off so he'd get tough with Doug."

Lantis took a step forward. His arms were out and to the side. "Hey, you got me all wrong."

He took another tentative step, and Kate did something I'd never seen except in movies. She put her left thumb on the pistol hammer, cocked it, extended her right arm, and fired. She blew the crown off a rock not ten feet behind Ed Lantis. Molly hit the deck and rolled over. Lantis merely sat. Stunned. His smirk vanished.

Kate's cheeks glowed like someone else's might glow at an outdoor wedding, the afternoon filled with love. She said, "We're going to talk, or I'm going to shoot you. I'll shoot you both. I don't care anymore."

Twenty-one

Lantis seemed to resign himself to having a conversation; there is no ignoring bullets. He leaned back against a slab of black-streaked stone and picked at his teeth with the folded cover of a pack of matches. Bits of gold flashed. Kate held the pistol level, pointed at Lantis.

Molly was planted on the ground, bug-eyed. She stared at Kate like a true believer. Kate's left thumb cocked the hammer a second time.

I said, "Don't worry, he'll talk." This was my way of telling Kate to calm down, to take it easy.

Lantis said, "I'll talk, college boy, because I've known Katy since before you were born." He nodded to her. "You know, your brother knew he was a screw up. He'd get in a jam, and after you got him out of it, he'd moan about it for weeks. He knew he'd bled Garston Timber, though you and I both know it wasn't that huge a deal, in the bigger picture. But Joe always saw himself in the center of everything, including GT."

Molly's body quaked. She looked away from everybody, head down, hidden under the flag of brassy hair.

Lantis said, "When Joe and B-B came to me for money, Joe said he was going to surprise you. He claimed he could sell ten bags for two hundred grand, one level below the street. I didn't know if Joe was full of it or not. It didn't matter. My investment was for ten I get twenty. Anyway, the idea was Joe would end up with a hundred and ten, and

174

B-B seventy. He said he planned on putting fifty back into Garston Timber, as a surprise for you."

From under her hair, Molly said, "Bullshit. Joe wanted to get back together. We were going to take that hundred grand and go somewhere. Like maybe New Zealand. Why the hell you think I went up there in the middle of the night? Why the hell you think I tried to hitch-hike to the ranch after I got a flat?"

Lantis cracked a superior smile. He said, "The love of his sister was no small thing. Maybe Joe thought he could buy it."

Kate fired over Ed's head. The sound ricocheted farther and farther up the granite on the other side of the Sulphur stream. Molly hit the deck again.

Kate said, "Cut the crap. B-B says you were at Doug's. I want an explanation."

Lantis said, "What I'd like to know is, where is your loyal servant now?"

"What you'd like, and what you're going to get, are two different things. Now either you talk, or I start blowing holes in the white bags."

Lantis looked more weary than upset. "All right, all right all ready. I was protecting my investment."

Kate raised her arm, and fired. A bullet ripped open a pack of cocaine. White powder sprayed about.

Molly whipped her hair toward Lantis. She said, "He was her *brother*. Don't you even get it? Don't you see she'll blow this whole deal if you keep acting like an asshole?"

Lantis continued as if Molly weren't there. "Joe was supposed to go make copies of the map, put notes on 'em, and mail one to Guaymas. I didn't think much about it. Then about nine o'clock, B-B calls asking if I know where Joe is. B-B was out cuttin' with a crew all day. He didn't get back till late. Joe hadn't come back from town, and it didn't take a genius to figure that meant he'd gone to Art's. We got worried because the more Joe drank, the more he might open his fat mouth."

Lantis looked to Kate. This time his smile was menacing. "Do you think that's a fair statement?"

"It's fair," She said. "Go on."

"About midnight, B-B calls to say Joe still hasn't shown. I told B-B to stay at your place, in case Joe arrived. I drove over the hill to look for him. I found him standing next to a cop car, not far from where he later got hit. Doug Kolatch had been coming up Highway One, making his rounds, and almost hit Joe on a curve. Joe had been walking up the road blitzed. When I got there, he was mouthing off. Doug said he was going to take him in. Well, with my truck behind the cop car, we were a hazard. I talked Doug into us going up on the fire road, to see if we could get Joe to straighten up. I made it a personal favor thing. I thought Doug just wanted to scare Joe, then he'd let me take him home."

A gust of wind fanned Molly's hair and momentarily lifted Lantis' brown ponytail. Kate held the gun with both hands. She let it rest against her belly.

Lantis said, "We went up on the dirt road, and pulled over where there was room for two cars."

Molly and I looked at each other—quick glances.

Lantis said, "Doug lets him out of the back, and your brother starts lecturing him on the evils of policing, cussing him out. By then, Doug has had it. He tells Joe to turn around and put his hands on the hood of the cop car. I don't want him to take Joe in, because there'll be a map in one of his pockets. So I tell Doug if he'll let your brother go, I'll give him framing lumber for the house he and his wife were planning."

"You out and out offered Doug Kolatch a bribe?" Kate waved the steely pistol. "You're really that stupid?"

"I had to do *some*thing. But it didn't work. He put a hand on Joe's back. Doug turns to me and says, 'What's going on? Why all this interest in Joe at two in the morning?'"

Kate said, "*Shit.*"

Lantis said, "I told him I was trying to help an old friend of the family. I could tell Doug knew I was lying. Then your drunk-ass brother runs down the hill into the brush. I told Doug I'd cover the highway, and he could work down from up top. That'd put Doug on foot. I was thinking Joe wasn't so dumb after all. I could catch up to him on the highway, get the map and deliver him to Kolatch. The worst that could happen was he'd get arrested, and you'd bail him out. But just as I'm starting my truck, I hear a car skid. Just skidding. No horn, nothing else. I race up the road, get down to the highway. Coming around the first turn I see Joe on the ground, in front of a car's headlights. There's a guy near him, on his hands and knees. I flip a U-turn. Almost hit Doug head-on, who must've run back to his car when he heard the skidding. I drove straight home. I called B-B, told him to stay put."

Molly had curled into a ball. She wasn't crying or showing any emotion. She was knotted up chastely on the ground. A wet spot showed in the crotch of her jeans.

Lantis said, "That's how it happened."

Kate said, "Shut up for a minute."

I sat there in a strung-out wonderment. I'd been aiming to find a murderer, aiming to gain glory, and now I hear, from someone who was there, Joe's death was an accident brought on by his own impulsive act. Lantis' story meshed with everything I knew. It explained Molly's seeing the police car, and Lantis not seeing her because she would have been running up the hill while he was driving around to fetch Joe down on the road. My hunch was Kolatch hadn't seen Molly coming up from the side. In his rush, car windows shut because it was past midnight, he wouldn't have heard her scream over the roar of his engine and tires as he sped away.

Now I had no reason, other than Kate, for being there.

Joe Garston had been a drunk, killed by a drunk.

Kate said, "Did Doug have maps on him when you and Bob went to his place?"

Lantis unsnapped the left pocket of his flannel shirt and took out a folded sheet of dirty white paper. He said, "Map, date, time. Brilliant Joe was walking up the highway, drunk, with this sticking out of his back pocket." Lantis rolled the piece of paper into a ball and tossed it at Kate.

I darted in front of her and caught the paper. I unfolded it and saw it was as Lantis described.

He twisted the ends of his dark mustache. "I've got an investment that was compromised. I plan on making it pay off."

Kate said, "Screw your investment. Let me think."

She closed her eyes and rubbed them with her left hand. This was the first time Kate seemed to waver, her first sign of mental fatigue.

I trained my gaze on Lantis, making sure he didn't move.

Kate adjusted the aim of the pistol. Her voice dry, she said, "You got anything to add to what Ed just said? You, Miss Pissed-Your-Pants?"

Molly looked up. "Not that I can think of."

Kate said, "Then get out of here, you little bitch. You and I are going to have to make a settlement, but I'm not going to look at you any more than I have to. So move your skinny ass out of my sight."

Molly got up, trying her best to meet Kate's heat with some of her own. Molly took her time knocking dust off her jeans. She styled her hair with fingers. Then Molly impressed the hell out of me. She said, "Can I take one? It'll keep me quiet."

"Sure, by all means." Kate was so pissed that for half a second I thought she might shoot Molly for the pure pleasure of it. But she motioned with the pistol. "Take one. It's more than you'll ever get out of Garston Timber."

Molly went to the unzipped black duffel sack, found a bag of cocaine that was to her liking, and headed back the direction she and Lantis had come from. Molly was so skinny that from afar she seemed to be speeding away on stilts.

Kate said, "Bobby should get what he went in for. I'll get it to him. I'm here for Joe's."

Her words caused me to look at her, and wake up to the fact that I was in the mountains with nine plastic bags of cocaine and two people pissed off and at odds with each other. I said, "B-B's finances are of no interest to me. And your brother's gone. His financial dealings don't matter, either."

Lantis chuckled, flashing gold. "Fucking college boy."

Kate said, "I just want to make things whole. These are supposed to be worth twenty thousand each, right? One equals your projected payout." Eyes and cocked gun on Lantis, Kate said, "I'm collecting for Joe and B-B. We gave one to Molly for insurance. I'll take that from my side."

Lantis said, "Don't get fancy, Katy. We got a whole new deal if I'm not getting cash."

She said, "You said your investment was for a loan of ten you get twenty."

Lantis hit the stone behind him with an open hand. His jaw was tight, his words hisses. "*Quit*, goddamn it. I've taken a lot of risks. I helped keep B-B away from the law. I helped out your asshole brother as much as you did. I wasn't even supposed to see this stuff. Now I got to find a buyer, something out of my orbit, because your brother screwed everything up. This is a totally different deal now."

Another shot blasted the granite behind him. Lantis hit the deck.

Lantis said, "Fuck." He spoke slowly, somehow rubbing in the word as if poking a wound. "Fuck, fuck, fuck." He twisted the ends of his dark mustache. "I don't know what the game is here, but it's just about over. We can cut a deal that's fair to all parties. I get three for making this deal happen in the first place. Without me we wouldn't be here, and now I got to risk my ass selling the shit. You get six, three for you and three for B-B. Try anything else, we got trouble."

I drank water. Kate drank water. Ed lit a cigarette. I screwed the cap on the canteen and tossed it to Lantis. He caught it, then snuffed out his cigarette on the ground.

Kate said, "Two is fair, because you're right, the deal changed. Now you got to move the product. Take two and follow Molly. She'll be on the way to wherever you left your truck."

Lantis shook his head. "Three. That's where we're at."

Kate said, "I could take them all and you couldn't do a goddamn thing about it."

Lantis said, "Okay, fine. I could burn down your house. I could pay some dope grower to burn down your mill. I could do this, I could do that. Cut the crap. We're equal partners here."

Kate said, "Two, you bastard. You only put in ten grand. You get two. We're *finis*."

This struck Ed Lantis as funny. He'd been swallowing water and laughed so hard he had to spit it out. He said, "*Finis!*" And resumed cackling. This made Kate laugh. The thought occurred that we were one turn of events from me becoming the odd person out.

Ed coughed, wiped his mouth. He was still laughing. He said, "Okay, Katydid. We're *finis*. But at three-three-three."

Lantis screwed the cap back on the metal canteen. As he set it on the ground, I scooped up the half-zipped duffel back and took off running.

Behind me I heard, "Jeff! Honey! What're you doing?"

About two seconds later the gun fired. It stopped me. I turned and saw Kate trying to wrestle the big Colt 45 from Lantis' arm; he must have snatched it from her. She bit into his wrist. Lantis dropped the pistol and tripped sideways, holding his right wrist. Kate picked up the pistol.

I took off running again, clamping the duffel bag between my left hand and inside elbow like a football player galloping in the open field. Turning some with a turn in the land, glancing back I saw Kate point the gun at Lantis. Lantis raised his hands—then ran after me.

I raced through boulders near Sulphur Creek. I went around a boulder as large as a car and sprinted upstream. Lantis was tracking me, somewhere in the rocks. My pumping arms and legs banged granite, though I didn't feel it. The reeking Sulphur water seemed to bounce up and down to my right. I ran as hard as I could, chasing my chance to do something important, running through wilderness carrying dope to atone for the chicken-shit manner in which I'd been cruising through life. Everything grew familiar, as though I'd been there before. I remembered taking the same strides, though it seemed ages ago. Every individual flitting piece of the landscape was preternaturally clear, the contours and starkness of the rocks, the green tint of the streambed. Everything I passed had a charged, bold luminosity.

As though waking from a dream, I skidded into a gigantic, egg-shaped boulder. To my left was a high rock wall. There was no possibility of getting over it. To my right was a narrow, slanted ledge that ran above the Sulphur-smelling chugging water. I had no choice. I sprinted on it past the water-stained face of the boulder. I took about five fast strides, and slid into another stone wall. About a hundred feet tall, down its middle gurgled a foamy waterfall.

To three sides of me was stone. The stream, twelve feet across, was too wide to jump across. Plus I saw that wouldn't lead past the extended stone wall. I remembered the bone-handled switchblade Lantis used to slit ropes. I remembered the deft manner with which he'd wielded it.

Déjà vu washed through me again. I remembered each second from having lived it before. I tried to steer my mind to the luminous clarity I'd experienced just seconds ago, to help me think straight, but this was overridden by fear. I went to the base of the rock wall and wedged the black duffel bag between large stones. Ed Lantis would be there any second. The granite seemed to close in all around me.

I went to the egg-shaped boulder that rose well above my height, and focused on the narrow ledge of orange, mineral-water-stained rock that would allow passage. The rushing water suddenly sounded louder. I thought of Joe Garston's last moments, blurry dark flashes while stumbling through brush down the steep hillside. The asphalt coming at him like a solid black wall—and he's gone.

A high-top tennis shoe probed the slick rock. I watched that and nothing else. The shoe pushed down on rock and as that foot took weight and Lantis emerged around the corner I bulled my shoulder into him. This drove us airborne. Lantis caught the collar of my shirt with one hand and his other hand lost hold of the switchblade. We hit water.

The stream was neck high. His head rose through the surface of the water and I punched him across the right ear with my good left hand. His head swayed away from me. I swung at him again, but Lantis spun away and cracked me solidly with his elbow. Out of old habit I hit him with my right hand, but it was only half a hand; it slid across Lantis' face without impact. He knocked me backwards with a straight-on punch and next thing I knew two hands clamped around my throat. These were hands that had set many a choker on logs. I headed down.

I swung, but my punch was underwater and had no power. I used my hook hand to get hold of his ponytail. I yanked it as hard as I could. I was going to pull him off his feet. I did, but his legs swung forward and wrapped around me and his thumbs drove deeper into my windpipe.

I took in bitter water, then lost my air. I pulled at his hair. It had no effect. I kicked, driving his body back, but Lantis' grip stayed locked. I needed air. Panic set in.

The bones of his fingers pressed into my gullet. Water bubbled all around me. I punched underwater but hit nothing. I tried to twist out of his grip. I began to see pictures: the cabin Mom and I lived in; Debbie Allen, the first girl I fell for; a picnic table at Lions Club Park. More pictures flipped past, removing me from the present. It seemed like I was looking up at the pictures, and I heard the distant, strange sounds of a music box. I recognized the melody, though it seemed I'd heard it thousands of years ago. There was no mistaking that melancholy sound. When your time comes, don't expect Gideon's trumpet.

There was a flickering, like lights blinking off and on during a thunderstorm. The pictures slowed. Their sharpness faded. Something innate brought my right arm up and my pincer hand, thumb and forefinger, found the base of his Lantis' neck, and my own neck twisted and broke his hold on it. An energy I can only describe as an animalistic shot of strength rumbled through me. I was going to kill Ed Lantis. The hand that had palmed basketballs by the hour and spent thousands of hours working for sport now engaged in killing Ed Lantis. Ed's hands were off me and went around his own neck, trying to remove mine. My hands squeezed like wringing water out of a wet towel. Every last drop. Ed Lantis let go. His hands drifted to his sides. This woke me to the fact that I didn't need to kill him. I could drag him ashore. I pushed him sideways—and heard an echoing *thump*.

Ed Lantis crumpled forward, almost like he was hugging me. I pushed him away. I rose through the water.

Breaths raced in and out in short shallow pants. I could only see a couple of feet. Everything looked wavy. My legs brought me to the granite bank. My forehead fell onto rock. Fighting for breaths, I looked up and made out Kate. She was kneeling, hands pressed to her cheeks. Her grandfather's pistol rested on the damp granite in front of her. I looked back and saw Lantis floating, stomach down, in pinkish water.

I looked at Kate again, only then seeing B-B Stiving beside her. He was lathered in sweat like a draft horse after labor, his face so red he looked like he might have a heart attack.

B-B said, "I had to. He wouldn't have stopped."

I managed, "No. No." I don't know if I was shaking my head, though I think I was. I fought for air, and said, "He gave up. Didn't you see it? He let go."

I blacked out for a few seconds.

Next thing I remember is blinking and seeing Lantis again. The milky pink water surrounding him was spreading toward me. I scrambled onto the bank, coughing, spitting, my hands on wet stone. I didn't look at Kate, or B-B, or the water.

Still panting, I got out, "Couldn't you see he gave up? He let go of me."

B-B said, "I know Ed. He would've killed you, man."

Kate whispered, "I'm a little teapot."

Twenty-two

Ly clothes and shoes were sopping wet. I was numb with shock.
His body curled forward, face underwater, Lantis turned a
slow circle, spreading a trail of blood. The stream's pool was the color
of weathered brick.

B-B said, "When I got to my truck, I couldn't drive off. I knew Ed
would get nasty. I couldn't let him mess with you. Joe and Doug are
already dead. It was already too much."

Kate nodded. Her brows were crunched together. Her hair, damp
from waterfall spray, was turning into a nest.

B-B said, "I don't know what Ed told you, but before Doug and
I got wrestling over the map, he pointed at Ed and said Joe would
be alive if Ed hadn't thrown him down the hill. I didn't tell you last
night, because I didn't want to stir up any new trouble. I didn't think
it would help anything."

Kate's face went flat, expressionless. When she spoke, she sounded
like only a small part of her was there with B-B Stiving and me. "Ed
pushed Joe down the hill?"

B-B said, "Not directly. They were arguing. Ed slapped your
brother, spun him around, hard like, and lost hold of him. Joe went
flying down the hill. That's what Doug said. It makes sense. Ed was
always a hot head."

I looked to the water. Ed Lantis was sinking, slowly, like a log.
Right then I understood what B-B had shouted the day before: I was

185

glad it was someone else, and not me, who took the bullet. I tried to gather thoughts. I didn't feel a need to talk. My head dropped to granite.

I heard Kate pace back and forth over pebbles and grit. She said, "We can't change anything. I wish we could, but we can't." Her feet ceased crunching the sandy grit. "We're moving on. We have to. Did they get wet?"

B-B said, "I don't see the bag. It's not by the water."

I said, "It doesn't matter anymore."

I looked up. B-B stepped forward, picked up the gun. He wiped its handle back and forth across his jeans and then, balancing it on his palm, tossed it into the Sulphur stream.

I said, "The dope doesn't matter."

Kate said, "Jeff, Honey, you're not yourself." She came to me, kneeled and stroked my hair. "What's done is done. We can't change it, but we can pick up the pieces and turn it into something good. Between back taxes, and two loans I got to roll over, there's fifty-five thousand in bills facing the company, first of the year. Try to see it from my side."

B-B said, "It's just too late, man. The cops will only bring trouble."

Operating on a kind of ethereal, automatic pilot, I got up and skated around the egg-shaped boulder. I went to the crevice and worked the duffel bag free. I came back along the ledge without thought or hesitation. Kate stood up. She looked right at me. Her intensity, her pride, her pain, her sensuality, all were present. Still, I couldn't see it from her side.

B-B said, "Everything's cool. They're still dry."

Kate said to me, "You should sit down. You don't look so good."

I saw the dark hair framing round brown eyes, the long neck and aristocratic bones of Kate's face. I walked right past her and B-B Stiving. I'm sure they thought I was leading the march out. I don't know where the energy came from, but I broke into a run, gaining speed, again cradling the duffel bag like it was a football.

Kate shouted, "Jeff! Jeff!"

I heard her steps sliding over rock behind me.

B-B shouted, "Hey man, stop! You don't even know your way out of here."

Kate's voice blasted, "Let's talk about it!" A couple of seconds later, she screamed, "Goddamn you, stop!"

I was afraid to stop, because Kate might have talked me out of leaving. I didn't quit running till after I was in the trees and far enough away I was sure Kate and Stiving had given up trying to catch me. Pearly light fell in slanting shafts between long dark branches. The light seemed to have texture and its own murmuring, loving sound. For a few moments I heard bits of the music box I'd heard underwater. The notes drifted away. I thought about how every day is different from the day before, and every hour is different, too. I heard birds but didn't see them. I drank from a shiny rivulet that seemed to spring from the ground the moment I was thirsty. I realized I'd lost chunks of time. I remembered my cell phone, but of course it was dead.

I walked for maybe two hours. From a ridge I saw the sun heading west, and followed, knowing that eventually I would reach if not the highway, some kind of road. I came upon a sunny clearing. Using the duffel bag for a pillow, I stretched out and closed my eyes. I fell into a fitful sleep. I dreamed I wrestled a bear. I woke with a start when the bear, in one chomp, bit off my right hand. I didn't know where I was or how I'd gotten there. I stood, looked around, waited for my thoughts to jell. My clothes had dried except for a few patches that were still damp though not cold. My face hurt. My neck hurt. I didn't mind. I was alive.

The sun was present as pinpoints of light filtering through trees. I walked toward the light. After about an hour I heard a vehicle but could not see it. Maybe twenty minutes later I was beside Highway 101, walking south with my thumb out. I didn't want a driver to see what I looked like, as it might dissuade him, or her, from pulling over. If B-B and Kate somehow showed up, I was going to lose them in the woods again. I was hardly aware of the duffel bag filled with cocaine. When a guy pulled over and asked where I was going, I said the town of Sunset. I climbed into his truck. The driver looked at me funny but pulled back onto the road. In appearance he reminded me of the crabby fellow wearing a Peterbilt baseball cap the morning of the senator's arraignment. He had the same facial thickness and puffy eyes that inferred a too-fond relationship with beer. The same look of aging early from that and hard labor. Only this fellow was friendly to near jolly. The inside of his truck cab smelled of hamburgers and French fries. It smelled terrific.

We whizzed past darkening trees. He said, "What brings you down to Sunset?"

I said, "I'm going to see a man about a horse."

The driver nodded, conceding my reason for going to Sunset was none of his business. He said, "I'm Walt, by the way. I'm going to San Francisco to see my brother. Straight shot from Crescent City. I need somebody to help me stay awake."

"I'm Jeff. Thanks for the ride."

Walt reached over to shake. I semi-waved my half hand. Walt said, "Sorry. I didn't see it." He kind of cleared his throat, then wiped his nose. "No offense, but you don't look so good. You all right?"

"It's been a tough day."

I think he was waiting for me to explain. About a minute passed before he pointed out a patch of trees dying from beetle infestation.

Walt said, "You get in on those early enough, there's good money to be had. You can get the wood for free if you provide cleanup and haul away. You're doing them a favor."

I nodded but was only half listening. Drifting, I wondered where Kate was, wondered where Molly was, and wondered if B-B Stiving was still going to make a run for Canada. Once I told Sheriff Niles what had happened, the clock would be ticking on all three of them.

Walt woke me when we were about ten miles north of Sunset. I'd slept three hours. It was dark outside the whirring pickup truck. My head was nestled in the corner where the passenger seat came near the door. The duffel bag was wrapped tight in the crook of my right arm.

I said, "I guess I wasn't much help keeping you awake."

Walt said, "Forget it. I'm going to get some gas up here. Just tell me where you want me to drop you."

"Thanks. I'll get something to eat and take a pee."

I worked my left hand into the front pocket of my jeans. The bills I strained out were wrinkled, and a little damp. The truck pulled into a Rotten Robbie gas station.

I handed Walt a wrinkled fifty. He shook his head. I said, "I've been giving away fifties for a week and a half. Don't stop my fun now. Take two and I'll be rid of them that much faster."

I untangled another wrinkled greenback from the wad.

Walt said, "I don't think I want to know where these came from."

"Not a problem. I'll go get us something to eat."

I walked away from the truck. Walt climbed out and around to the gas pumps, eyed me keeping the black duffel bag with me. I was sore from the fight with Lantis and riding in the truck. I went inside the mini mart, peed and washed up, taking only a gander at my swollen nose, with a bumpy red tip, the swollen left cheek and the general look of dissipation I saw in the mirror. I patted my face with paper towel, left the restroom. I went to go ask Walt what he wanted to eat. Heading toward the glass doors, I saw that he had split.

I don't think Walt wanted anything to do a stranger looking like hell, clinging to a duffel bag and giving him two damp, crinkled fifty-dollar bills. I didn't blame him. I bought water, beef jerky and string cheese, and went out to the highway. I stuck out my thumb. I decided if no one picked me up after about fifteen minutes I was going to go inside and ask the kid clerk to call the Sheriff's office. I was going to tell him to say I needed to be picked up because I was carrying a hundred and eighty thousand dollars' worth of cocaine. It would have made the kid's month.

I'd turned to do just that when a Honda Accord swerved off the road. I saw it, but assumed the Honda was going to Rotten Robbie's for gas or food. The car's horn tooted. The right-side window slid down. The car lazed forward.

A friendly, confident voice said, "What are you doing out here?"

I stepped toward the open window. Looking inside, I saw Anne Simpson, the clerk on duty when I bailed out Watkins, later my dance partner at Art's, and later in mourning while on duty when I'd popped in to look over my stolen notebook.

I said, "I'm not sure what I'm doing out here. I'm kind of winging it. No, I'm definitely winging it."

She leaned over and tilted her head, trying to get a better look at me. Anne said, "Are you drunk?"

"I'm so tired I feel drunk."

The door unlocked with a *click*. Anne said, "Get in. I'll drive you to your car."

I said, "Oh, crap. I forgot about my car."

I got in the Honda Accord. I freed myself from the duffel bag by setting it on the backseat. Anne put on her left blinker, looked around to be safe, and pulled onto Highway One.

She said, "You don't look so good."

"I wish people would quit saying that."

Anne said, "I'm going to take you home for some coffee. Maybe you can tell me what's going on."

"First I got to take a shower and eat. Sorry if that's pushy, but I'm having trouble keeping my head straight."

Anne drove. I chewed beef jerky. I wondered if this was what a boxer felt like after fifteen rounds.

At Anne's house, a mile south of Rotten Robbie's, then inland and uphill under trees, she offered coffee, snacks, even dinner. I asked if I could take a shower. Her house, like most of the older ones in the area, was once a summer place. It had two modest bedrooms with a toilet, sink and shower between them. I stayed in the shower until the hot water ran out. God that warm water felt good. After I turned it off, Anne tapped on the door. She told me there were clothes for me in the guest bedroom, to the right.

On the bed, which was covered with a blue bedspread, were a neatly folded long-sleeved T-shirt, red with white sleeves and *Phillies* printed in cursive across the chest, underwear that was too small, but beggars can't be choosers, socks and hiking shorts. They were clean clothes. Men's clothes.

I entered the living room tugging down the shorts, and sat on a beige couch. Anne was in a brown Barcalounger with her feet kicked up. She didn't look relaxed, or like she was expecting a sociable chat. She hadn't lighted a cozy fire in the brick fireplace.

Clearly referring to the clothes I had on, Anne said, "Don't ask. It's off limits. I don't know why I just don't throw all his stuff away."

I said, "Not a problem."

Anne said, "Correct. But I looked in your duffel bag. That's a problem. I'm an officer of the court. I have to turn you in."

"I understand."

Anne sighed. She said, "I want to know what's going on with you, and I don't."

I oozed sideways along the couch. The warm water had relaxed me. "Good. I'll tell Niles everything in the morning."

Anne said, "Listen. I'm not comfortable with nine bags of cocaine in my living room."

"You could put them in the trunk of your car."

Anne said, "Yeah, right."

I closed my eyes, trying to remember where I'd left my car. I thought maybe in Sacramento, then knew that wasn't right. I remembered once taking an hour to park for a Kings basketball game against the Warriors, which made me realize I wasn't thinking straight. My shut eyes crunched together, in spasms. I told myself to let go, to not think.

Mid-morning. Blue jays hopped across a railing at the back porch, snapping up little chunks of bread Anne had set out for them. Smells of coffee and hotcakes wafted from the kitchen. I stood, stretched, and remembered Anne pulling over in her Honda, the window going down. She must have seen me stretching, because Anne came into the living room. She held a cup of steaming tea.

Anne said, "I called the Sheriff."

"What did he say?"

"He said, 'Okay.'"

"That's it?"

"Well, I did mention I was bringing you in with a duffel bag full of cocaine. I thought it would whet his appetite."

I said, "Something tells me Niles never lacks an appetite."

Anne said, "Pancakes are warm in the oven." Anne turned, steam trailing from her cup, and headed into the kitchen.

We left half an hour later. On curves I saw great views of the Pacific Ocean. I recognized where we were, a few miles north of Garston Ranch Road. It struck me that I wanted to do something before talking with Niles and setting the police in motion.

"Anne, I can't thank you enough. I was really out of it last night."

She said, "You told me I was great, just before you conked out for twelve hours. You said it three times. That'll count as a thank-you."

"I need to ask one more favor. Could you take me to the house Marci and Allan Watkins are renting for the month? I feel like I should fill him in."

Anne's hair was dangling long and straight that morning. She shook it. "So you want him to know what I don't?"

I said, "That sounds bad. I just feel a need to tell him what happened. He's innocent of everything except being a fool. Okay, drinking and driving, but mostly an old man who stupidly flirted with a young woman."

Anne said, "You really expect me to... Wait a second, are you a good liar?"

"Unfortunately, I've become proficient at it."

Anne said, "Okay, you get Watkins if you promise to tell the Sheriff you came knocking at my door in the middle of the night. Don't tell him I pulled over and offered you a ride. Let's agree on four in the morning. Okay? You Googled my address. You asked me to take you in. You'd been drinking, and you were a mess. If you can promise to do that, I'll take you to see Watkins."

"Not a problem."

Twenty-three

I knocked on the door of the stately house Senator and Mrs. Watkins rented every September. The senator answered. Soon as he saw me, he looked behind him. He said, "Son. Hey. It's a hell of a surprise." His cheeks were bright with drink. "*Honey*," he called, his voice rising with discomfort. "We have a visitor."

I said, "It's good to see you, sir."

Marci arrived, looking fresh as always. She invited me in. They both shook the outstretched left hand I offered. Clutched under my right arm was the black duffel bag. I sat in the rocking chair near the fireplace. They'd burned cedar the night before and fragrant chips of it littered the slate hearth. My right hook hand clamped the duffel bag. Some form of glance was likely exchanged between Marci and Watkins, because without words she left the room. No staff were present, no tough guy to keep the media or meddlers like me away.

Watkins sat in his favorite chair. He took a quick slug of gin. "What've you been up to, son?" His eyes darted about. It occurred to me that Marci might be calling the police.

"I've been working the case." I set the dark duffel bag on my lap and waited for him to ask about it. "I've been working it on my own."

To my surprise, Marci re-entered the room. She carried two suitcases. Her steps were purposeful.

Watkins said, "I guess you saw the papers. Or online? We leaked it to cushion the coverage." He took another sip of his drink. It was peaceful in that airy wood house. Watkins said, "Tom Marquardt pleads it tomorrow morning. I don't have to be there, which makes it easier for all parties. Involuntary manslaughter. No drunk driving because their machine was months past its recertification date. I lose my license, get a fine, probation, and a hundred hours of community service."

He saluted me with his glass and shot me a smile that must have hurt because it disappeared with an audible snap of his jaw. "Cheers."

My return smile came easily. Ever since waking, I'd felt better by the minute. I lifted the duffel bag, let it rest on my lap again. "If you're in the clear with drunk driving, you don't have to plead guilty to anything. You told me you were innocent. Now I know you are."

"What I am," Watkins said, then cleared his throat. "What I am, is glad to be going home. We'll issue a statement tomorrow after court. I'm dropping out of the race. Let someone else worry about the people of the ninth district."

He sucked the last drops from the glass tumbler. His face was a mix of flaming cheeks, bloodshot eyes, buttery chin and yellow beneath his eyes. It was hard to witness, knowing that only two weeks before he'd been a striding lion on the floor of the California state senate.

Watkins stood, hitched khaki pants over his gut. He half-staggered to the kitchen area. Marci appeared from the hallway carrying a cardboard box filled with papers. She set the box on the tile entryway and disappeared again.

Watkins dumped half-melted ice in the sink, filled the tumbler with fresh cubes from the refrigerator dispenser, and mixed another gin and tonic. While he did this, I rehearsed my triumphant words telling Watkins he could give retaining his beloved senate seat another shot.

Watkins said, "There's a right way to grow old and die. I've come to see that."

Marci appeared with another cardboard box. "Allan, don't be melodramatic. You're just retiring. People do it all the time."

He said to me, "You want a drink?"

"No, thanks. By the way, where's my buddy Lee Welty? I thought he'd be here spewing bullshit."

This brought another sallow grin from the old senator. "I let him go. You know what? He asked for a severance bonus, even though his contract was week-to-week. I reached into my pocket and gave him my spare change."

We laughed over that. Watkins brought his drink to the living room. I set the duffel bag containing a hundred and eighty thousand dollars' worth of cocaine on the wood floor. Marci reappeared. She quietly set down a computer case. I rubbed the ends of my half hand against my sore side. I looked to the high, sloped ceiling. It had been years since I'd felt like a winner. I wasn't dead and the senator was near blameless in Joe's death. And I still had my teeth.

Watkins sat at an angle across from me. He said, "Looks like somebody beat the crap out of you again."

I chuckled. "That's right. Somebody beat the shit out of me again. I'll get to that with the police. But I solved the case. You're innocent."

"I just told you. We agreed to a plea. There is no case."

I ran my fingers across the top of the dirty black duffel bag. "The reason Joe Garston died has nothing to do with your driving."

Senator Watkins' eyes flared, as if asking a question.

I patted the canvas bag. In an odd way it had become my companion. "I'm taking this from here to Sheriff Niles. I'll explain to him that this is why Joe died. I'll fill in the details for you if you want. I can explain everything."

Watkins got up from the chair. He paced one way, came back. I grabbed the duffel bag and set it next to the where he'd been sitting. "Joe was working a cocaine deal. You got in the middle of it when he tumbled down the hill. Pure bad luck. If you'll sit down, I'll explain it to you."

Watkins quit pacing. The wrinkles above his watery bloodshot eyes drew together. He was trying to clear his half-swacked brain.

I said, "Nine bags of cocaine. Take a look."

Watkins straightened his carriage. He went to the duffel bag, opened its top flap and looked inside.

I rose and went to the man I'd bailed out of jail. He had the same tics, the same objectionable habits, he was the same flawed human being who just happened to do more good deeds for California than I ever would.

I felt a kinship. Like Clint Sherman, Allan Watkins had become a kind of father figure, a man who had gone far in life, who people counted on, a man like I had never known as a boy.

I said, "After I tell Niles what happened, and how I got this, you're basically in the clear."

Senator Watkins nodded. He put a hand out, as if for quiet. He walked to the central hall that led to bedrooms. His voice was loud, clear. "Honey," he said. "*Honey!*" Watkins stepped down the hallway, out of sight. I heard him say, "Honey-Love, could you get Tom Marquardt on my cell? When I'm with him, use yours and get me Miss Beldon and Lee Welty. Tell them to wait for my call."

A heaviness fell upon my chest. I heard footsteps crossing wood. Senator Watkins returned to the living room. In about a minute he had sobered himself up. I figured he'd had a lot of practice.

Watkins said, "Thank you for bringing this to our attention. When you see Niles, tell him I'm available to answer questions as soon as my attorney arrives, which won't be till this evening at the earliest."

I said I would. My feet seemed planted in cement boots. What happened to my triumph?

I said, "Senator, you're probably going to pull yourself out of this, and win."

He said, "Thanks. You're the reason it's going to happen."

"It's good I found out who really killed Joe. It's good you won't have to drop out of the race."

Senator Watkins, revved by changed fortunes, strode toward me like a younger man. His right hand was outstretched. I didn't shake it.

"No, thanks."

The senator frowned, displaying that map of wrinkles that had expanded over the decades. He motioned to the duffel bag. He said, "You're going to the authorities and tell them about whatever made Garston fall in front of my car. You're going to do your civic duty, just like I'll do mine."

"You're right about doing our civic duty. Beyond that, I hope we have nothing in common. I'm leaving now."

A sadness crept across his face, joining the back-in-the-game energy that had cleared his head and sprung him into action. "Just tell the truth about Joe Garston to the police. Okay? Just tell them the truth."

I didn't answer. I didn't say goodbye. I scooped up the black duffel bag and left Senator Allan Watkins and the world of Sacramento politics behind.

Anne was parked facing downhill, ready to leave. I opened a back door of her Honda and deposited the duffel bag on the bench seat. Anne put her phone down as I got in.

"How'd it go?"

"It went. I told him what happened, just a summary. He was dropping out of the race, today. Now he's staying in."

Anne said, "Somehow, I'm not surprised." She started the engine, headed downhill. "I called the sheriff and told him we'll be a little late."

I'd accomplished what I wanted, knowing the truth about the death of Joe Garston, yet didn't feel good about any of it, not least that a man was dead and bloated in a foul-smelling creek out in the middle of nowhere. I had helped Senator Watkins but didn't feel good about that, either. Anne had her blinker going. She pulled out left and we headed south on Highway One.

Anne said, "Should you call a lawyer, before you meet with the sheriff?"

"No."

"You sure?"

"I'm not going to call a lawyer."

Outside, incoming waves struck white rocks. I lowered the window and smelled the ocean. It helped revive me from the hollowness I felt after being with Senator Watkins. I said, "I just thought of something. When I posted bail, you said you'd seen me play. Where was it?"

"My older sister went to Sac State. When I was a senior in high school, the coolest thing in the world was to go to the big city for the weekend and stay in her dorm. I was on the team at Sunset High, so we went to watch Sac State games. You showed me how the star can be a team player. You never hogged the ball. You were my role model for sports when I was in high school."

"You make me sound kind of old."

"When I was seventeen, you *were* kind of old. You know, like twenty maybe?"

We passed Garston Ranch Road. I remembered my car was parked at Kate's. I was still a little loopy from almost getting killed and then walking for several hours. Anne drove through downtown Sunset. Anne, ever law-abiding, put her blinker on about a hundred yards before we reached the county center complex. We entered the parking lot. Nearest the building labeled Sheriff's Department, two patrol cars sat in designated slots.

Niles must have been watching through the glass doors. He emerged from the building before Anne parked. I took a slow, deep breath, got out, opened the back door and grabbed the black duffel bag. We met Sheriff Niles on the aggregate concrete in front of the building.

Niles grinned. I don't think it was insincere. He said, "Jeff Taylor, you come up here and raise nothing but trouble, and you still end up spending time with two of the most interesting women in Sunset County. Lucky man. No?"

A couple, arguing with each other over a parking ticket, came outside and walked past us.

Niles looked west, to the Pacific. He said, "Couldn't you just breathe in that sea air all day? Swallow it by the mouthful?" Niles enjoyed one breath. "Let's get on with it."

Niles pulled open the glass door, waited for Anne to enter first. I followed. Niles came in and was at my side, motioning for me to start down a hall. A few steps later, he stopped. Niles looked me over.

"You might consider finding yourself another line of work. You don't look so good."

Anne shot me a spirited glance. Niles caught it. He said, "Why you two so cozy? Anne, have you done something that means I'm going to have to fire you?"

Anne said, "I hope not."

I said, "Blame me. I showed up drunk at her place. Besides, she's the one bringing me in."

We started walking again. Niles' feet kind of shuffled over the square, tan-colored tiles.

Niles said, "You know what. I'm going to let you read him his rights. Any officer of the court can do it."

Anne grimaced. "Okay, Sheriff."

We reached the tall door with CONFERENCE painted on it in white. Niles turned the handle. Like before, he opened the door for Anne to enter, then me. Anne stepped inside and gasped. My gasp was right behind hers. Kate Garston sat at the long conference table next to a man in a suit and tie who I assumed was a lawyer. His hands were folded, resting on the table. Kate wore a white blouse and a long gray skirt. She didn't look at me. Hell yes I was scared. I'd broken the law about six ways. Nobody stood up or said anything. A deputy was there, too, one of the guys in uniform I'd seen outside the county center working crowd control the day I snatched Watkins from the press conference. He didn't look at Anne. He looked at a laptop screen. Next to his right hand were a ledger and a ballpoint pen.

Kate, her face half concealed by curly brown hair, said, "You don't have to worry. I told them how he was choking me when you got

Grandad's gun from my pack. I told them how you saved my life."

I couldn't think straight. Was I really being set up by a table full of locals?

Anne said, "I don't believe it." Then to me, in utter shock, "Should I believe it?"

I shook my head, *No*. My brain fogged over. I couldn't process what was happening.

Niles shuffled around to the head of the table. "We got a dessert platter coming from Perry's. My treat. A little of everything. They'll be here any second." Niles sat. He rocked forward and back. He seemed happy. He said, "It's been a messy couple weeks. But now that we're all together, I think we can straighten things out."

Sheriff Niles pointed to the deputy and said to me, "Mr. Taylor, give that bag to Deputy Price, will you please? And both of you take a seat, for goodness sakes. Take a seat and make yourselves comfortable."

Kate tried not to look at the black duffel bag filled with a hundred and eighty thousand dollars' worth of cocaine, and failed. I saw this was not lost on Sheriff Niles. I handed him the black duffel bag. Anne and I dropped onto adjacent wood chairs. They were hard. The back of mine seemed to poke into me. Everything was happening fast.

Kate said, "They'll understand, you were saving me."

Kate's lawyer's eyes didn't stray from his entwined fingers. "I remind you not to say anything we haven't already discussed. I hope I'm making myself clear."

Niles said, "We'll get to the bottom of this barrel. We'll all work together." Niles looked to Anne, who like Kate's attorney simply stared ahead. Niles said, "Give Mr. Taylor his rights. Kate already got hers a while ago. Price, you can start recording now on that little thing. Just don't screw it up."

Anne closed her eyes. She recited my constitutional rights, stopping herself a few times to ask me if I understood. Each time, I said, "Yes." I'd never heard the whole thing before. It took longer than I would have expected.

Niles said, "Anne, I'm officially putting you on leave. You're here as a witness, not a county employee. Price, record that, and read Ms. Anne Simpson her rights."

Anne gulped, tried her best to be stoic. I gave her hand an encouraging squeeze. Deputy Price recited Anne's rights. She said "Yes" in the same places I did. When Price finished, Sheriff Niles bumped the conference table with his bulk, causing everyone's attention to turn his way. A crisp knock came at the door.

Niles beamed. "Come on in!" He added, "That'll be the kids from Perry's. Don't miss the blueberry tarts—wow. We'll have a nice long chat. Clear things up."

Anne said, "I'm scared."

I said, "Of the three of us, you're the only one who hasn't done anything wrong."

A young woman wheeled in a cart, rather formal looking. Across its top were two round platters of assorted bakery treats. Their pleasant scents were completely out of place in that setting. Behind the young woman came a young man carrying a sack of bottles of flavored mineral water, Coke and 7-Up. The Sheriff looked like a proud host. The two kids from Perry's deposited the food and drink on the long table.

Niles said, "No reason we can't nosh while we talk."

I said, "I don't see a problem." I was regaining composure and thought the number one priority for me was to put Kate ill at ease.

Kate said, "They won't prosecute you. You don't need to say anything. You were just trying to save me."

Kate's attorney said, patiently, gently, "If you break our agreement one more time, I'll choose not to represent you."

Deputy Price's eyes stayed on the laptop. "Working fine."

In a half whisper, Anne said, "Make sure you save everything every couple minutes." She took a breath. "Wi-Fi cuts out sometimes on this end of the building."

Sheriff Niles nodded. "Thank you for that. It's just what I mean by working together."

He snatched a blueberry tart off the tray of sweet-smelling treats. It disappeared. Niles grabbed and downed what looked like a peanut butter cookie.

He said, "Come on, friends. Don't make me eat alone." Niles gave all of us one of his big Teddy Bear winks. He rubbed his hands together. "I'm hoping we can straighten things out before District Attorney Chapman returns from his mom's down in Sonoma. I want to give him a nice surprise."

Kate's attorney, eyes not moving from his entwined hands, sighed and shook his head.

Niles said, "Okay. Who wants to go first?"

Twenty-four

Sheriff Niles, and later District Attorney Chapman, and after that a team from the Federal Bureau of Alcohol, Firearms and Tobacco, straightened everything out. Kate ended up admitting it was B-B Stiving who shot Ed Lantis, but only after her lawyer had wrapped her lies in a package of mental duress over the death of her only, dearly beloved sibling, and a psychiatrist's report containing fancy terms for temporary insanity. These combined to legally distance Kate from the fact she'd jumped into a cocaine deal. That she'd never had the drugs in her possession was in her favor, and no charges against her were filed.

Once things calmed down, I realized I'd been batty myself in thinking Kate and I were falling in love, and equally batty in thinking she might fill the hole left inside me by my mom's deserting me for a life with Del Beverage in Alaska. That was an old wound that needed fresh examination.

B-B Stiving's pickup truck was found covered by freshly cut pine branches in dense forest, in Washington, twenty miles south of the Canadian border. It was never known if he crossed the border, though since he wasn't found in the U.S., it seems likely he did. To my knowledge he has never been heard from.

Molly didn't last through the weekend of the drug drop before she was caught and brought to Sunset for questioning. She was nailed for possession of cocaine, though as a first offender, and not yet a seller, her attorney got her probation, with a year living in a halfway house and holding down a steady job. Molly waitressed at Homer's Buffet, in Ukiah, where she provided free music on Friday nights.

Allan Watkins lost reelection by eleven percentage points. Once it came to light he had picked up a twenty-something woman hitchhiking before he hit Joe Garston—this while he drank from a pint of brandy—the goodwill of his constituents ran dry.

After the court stuff was done, wherein two judges chewed me out for withholding evidence, and for going with Kate to the cocaine drop, I was free. Sherman Investigations provided my legal counsel. Clint Sherman did not communicate with me, and the arrangements came via an intermediary. I didn't receive a bill. It wasn't until February that legal matters were cleared up.

I headed across America in my Jetta, chains and snow tires packed in the trunk. I took Highway 80 through Nevada to Utah, and continued east. The longer I was on the road, the people I encountered began to seem more interesting. I drove to Chicago, a miracle of tall buildings, stone and glass, sitting on the shore of a Great Lake. I was just past halfway across this extraordinary country. I was in no hurry. I was twenty-five years old and seeing everything with fresh eyes. At night I studied for the MCATs online.

I drove into a snowy New England. The landscape was wonderful, as were the people. I practiced for the spring MCATs every bit as hard as I'd once practiced with a basketball on hardwood courts. I traveled from town to town all over Vermont, New Hampshire and Maine, talking with people, hiking across fresh snow, staying in motels with Wi-Fi so I could study. I planned on becoming a pediatrician. And when I do, children will leave my office knowing they're okay, they are good, that someday they'll do something great.

About the Author

Scott Lipanovich lives in Santa Rosa, California. Stories of his have appeared in Ireland's *Fish Story Prize*, *The Seattle Review*, *Crosscurrents*, *Defiant Scribe*, *Abiko* (Japan), *Wild Duck Review*, *Ridge Review*, *Gold and Treasure Hunter Magazine*, *Summerfield Journal*, and several anthologies.

In film, Scott has worked with two Academy Award winners, and two multiple Emmy-winning producers.

If you enjoyed reading this book,
please consider writing your honest review
and sharing it with other readers.

Many of our Authors are happy to participate in
Book Club and Reader Group discussions.
For more information, contact us at info@encirclepub.com.

Thank you,
Encircle Publications

For news about more exciting new fiction, join us at:

Facebook: www.facebook.com/encirclepub

Twitter: twitter.com/encirclepub

Instagram: www.instagram.com/encirclepublications

Sign up for Encircle Publications newsletter and specials:
eepurl.com/cs8taP

CPSIA information can be obtained
at www.ICGtesting.com
Printed in the USA
BVHW080724290721
613100BV00003B/573